To Tim + Beth
The best friends are old friends
Phil Denkensteen, author
8/21/2022

Almost *Magic*

By Phil Finkelstein Copyright 2021, all rights reserved

Dedicated to our ever expanding universe: Louie, June, Alice, Rose, Tova, Ora, Ephraim, Kayla and our personal Super Nova Barb. Never stop exploring!

Marking Time

We stand at the shore
Our toes grasp the sand
Intertwined are our hands
As we gaze beyond-and
Years rush past.

As we gingerly, inexorably, move beyond
Approaching the final blue horizon
We sense its defining light.

We tighten our grip and fear not
Our Love shines ever bright
Our Love shines long into the night.
Pf 12-26-19

TABLE OF CONTENTS

Dedication iii
Poem: Marking Time v
Prologue 3

Part One: Almost There
  1. The Current Beginning 11
  2. A Break in the Action 27
  3. Sometimes, A Hot Shower is not Enough. 35
  4. Texas Hold It 41
  5. Deep in the Heart of Texas 49
  6. Go Fish 58
  7. Sisterly Talk 60
  8. Ann Comes to Town 66
  9. The Great Awakening 69
  10. Time to Go 73
  11. What You Don't See, is What You Get. 77
  12. They Go Bat Sh*t Crazy 82
  13. On the Road Again 88
  14. Texas is a BIG State. 90
  15. The Repair is in the Details 100

16. Tasting Another's Life 106
17. Proper Boundaries 116
18. Be Careful What You Ask For… 122
19. The End of the Beginning 129

Part Two: Almost Home
20. Then There Were Two. Sort Of. 137
21. Returning 145
22. Not Quite Paradise But Close Enough To Spit On It. 148
23. Getting Acclimated 152
24. Temple 154
25. Passing Time: Happy hour with the Neighbors 158
26. V Bar V 169
27. Jerome 186
28. The Routine 195
29. Another Nightly Routine 199
30. Friends of the Forest 200
31. The Door Bell Only Rings Once 206
32. A Good Day for a Hike 212
33. Sue Calls 218
34. Larry Comes Around 220
35. Ben and Larry Talk-Almost 226
36. A Little Night Magic 232
37. Almost But Not Quite There 243

Author's Note 252
Poem: Hiking on the Back Side 254

PART ONE

ALMOST THERE

Prologue

It was a cold day in November when they buried Ann, the leaf ground cover had already frozen enough to make a crunching sound when Ben walked on it. Left to their own devices, Ann and Ben would have preferred to be cremated and have the ashes spread on some beautiful spot that the two of them found meaningful over the years. Maybe Grand Marais or Sedona. Neither Ben nor Ann were big on cemeteries. (Why waste the space?) But the two of them had promised their religious daughter Esther that they would be buried in accordance with tradition. They joked that they wouldn't be around anyways, so who cares? Well, Ben did and right now it felt like a stone was tied onto his heart. Heavy and hurtful. Ben sighed and allowed himself to be guided by 2 of their adult children to the grave site which was already prepared. Their third child, Sue was already sitting in the mourners' row crying quietly apart from what was left of the family. 6 folding chairs for the mourners had been set up in front of the already dug burial site. The deep 8 foot by 4 foot hole was stark and unyielding. The 5 foot pile of dirt was a reminder to all where they would end up when they time had passed. Ben, still in shock, couldn't believe that Ann, his beloved Ann had been taken, NO SAY IT, died in her late 50s.

Because of the risk of freezing rain, a waterproof canopy protected the mourners. Ben looked up and was reminded of those times he and Ann used to walk in the rain. Intentionally. There was something special about being huddled together under a large golf umbrella. Ann often joked that the rain might wash and cleanse their souls. They had met at college on one of the rare days Ben deigned to eat his lunch at the Student Center. A very cute woman in her early 20's, she was sitting by herself in a corner. She was twirling her finger into her already curly dark hair while reading intently. Just as interesting was the thick book she was reading on the history of the Ottoman Empire. Later Ben learned she was reading it just for fun. What history major like Ben could resist that? While Ann could initially- Ben couldn't and Ben suffered through 3 whole wheat tuna fish sandwiches a week at the Center for 2 months before she agreed to go out with him. The rest was history but to this day, Ben still could not stomach a tuna fish sandwich-still Ann's favorite. (He had eaten them when they met hoping that Ann would realize he had the same good taste as her.)

2 years and 627 tuna fish sandwiches later, they married and time passed quickly. Their River of Life carried them through 4 homes, 3 children, death of all their parents, 5 jobs and so many of Life's rocks and challenges- it was impossible to keep track of them all. But the important notion was they traveled in that same life raft together, most of the time, happily. They shared beds, finances, doctors, meals, sick children, joys, disappointments, triumphs, sex, touch, talks, silences, holidays, funerals, divorces(their friends), all the individual pieces that together make up a full life and if one is lucky – a family. Ben realized he had been lucky enough to marry Ann and share their journey. Although it might be considered funny, they shared so many interests and hobbies together like history, current events, literature, music (especially Blues), nature, hiking- their friends called each of the two: Professor Wisenheimer- interchangeably. But it was the simple things that they really appreciated the most about each other. How they treated each other every day like her putting tooth paste on his tooth brush so he would be reminded about daily dental hygiene and his making her tea most every afternoon that made their relationship so special. (Ben was the first to admit

that Ann was much, much better at remembering to do the "little stuff." She was right it was the small things that show how much you care about someone and that you don't take them for granted. Now Ben would never be able to catch up.

In any case, the time had passed by so quickly. A quick blur if you looked back. But not today. Every minute seemed to take an hour. Ben still didn't understand why Ann's soul along with the rest of her body had departed several decades too soon. Ben had always thought he would go first. Guys usually do. Men when alone, joke that's because they can. Somewhat selfishly, he wished that had been the case here. Ben looked up at the temporary canvas ceiling and for a moment he could have sworn it was Ann floating but that just couldn't be. Ben looked again and Ann was gone. Forever. A wave of anguish passed through Ben's body and he sobbed. Esther patted his arm in support. Just like her mom.

The Rabbi cleared her throat- it was time to begin:

"Thank you all for coming. It's a big crowd in spite of the weather- Ann would have liked that. We are here today to lay Ann Joy Stein, Aleha ha-shalom (of Blessed memory) to rest far too soon.

Anne, oh what the heck, let's just call her AJ (she smiled) AJ was well known as a gentle force of strength and love to everyone she knew. But AJ was so much more:

AJ loved her work- Whether it was it was a high level job at United Healthcare or here at the toddlers' room, AJ was a thoughtful, generous hard worker who was never too busy to serve as some employee's mentor or remember someone's birthday. She was always there.

AJ loved her community- While many people talk about community, AJ actually lived it from being active in the League of Women Voters to volunteering for 13 years at the local school helping small children discover the joy of reading.

But most of all, AJ loved her family (The Rabbi paused) her children Esther, Larry and Sue including her beloved husband Ben, her Bashert (Hebrew for her intended one.)

AJ lived for her children, even working at the Temple early childhood center, taking leave from her chosen field as a corporate librarian, so she could be there with them in those important beginning years.

(The Rabbi paused again- now she was getting into what those in the Rabbi Trade called the vital statistics)

We can all see the results in their 3 children sitting here today:

Larry - a lawyer,

Esther- a MSW Social worker complete with 2 adorable grandchildren.

And the smartest of all- Sue who had the wisdom to relocate to Flo-Ri-Da many years ago. (Only a couple chuckles).

Then there was what's his name (More chuckles) Ben- Their's was a love for the ages. Even though they had been married for 36 years, I could still see them holding hands during religious services. Then again it might been Ann trying to keep Ben from sneaking off to get Starbucks coffee. (The most chuckles.)

Here the Rabbi sighed, loudly:

After being a Rabbi for 17 years, the truth is I still don't know why God pulls some of us away so early. To be honest, when I found out Ann had suddenly died, I swore (yes, even Rabbis know how) at God saying, you took the wrong person. You took my friend. It didn't make any sense to me. We are all here on earth for too short a period of time and why is it the good ones like Ann, who go first? Ann actively volunteered at the Temple and a lot in our community, who loved her husband, children and grandchildren, not necessarily in that order, but what better use can you make of her somewhere else?

The Rabbi paused again and looked at the crowd she decided to go for it, departing from her text:

"We may never understand the necessity of death but it is just part of our reality. What's God purpose in taking such as good soul as Ann is something our faith teaches us….(The Rabbi faltered, this was her friend after all and she wasn't going to phone it in - and after a couple of seconds, continued)… is why we must place our trust in-God. (She just couldn't think of anything else that was honest left to say.)

May Ann's memory continue to be a Blessing to all of us.

The Rabbi wiped a real tear from her eye, then continued:

At this time I would like to recite the Mourners' Kaddish which for over 1200 years, memorializes the departed, not in their name but instead by praising God."

But before they could get started, Ben heard something between a car horn and a cow being strangled- it oddly sounded vaguely like Green Sleeves. He turned in the direction of the noise, you couldn't quite call it music and there he spied Don marching stiffly towards them. Don, a friend since High School, was in full Scotch regalia including a tartan kilt and a tam hat in the middle of November!

"Am I too late? I had to repair my bagpipe at the last minute with duct tape. I just wanted to play my respects." Don being Don, had to show where his hedge trimmer had whacked the plastic bagpipe right before the funeral. Ben simply shook his head. Don usually meant well but didn't always do well. This was one of those latter times. Ben had looked for Don and his wife during the ceremony and wondered why he wasn't there. Don loved Ann and was devastated when she passed. Ben knew he was acting out his grief in a manner only Don could understand. Ben wasn't mad. Like Ann always used to say when confronted with Don's latest caper: There's a right way and Don's way. But Ben was just too emotionally exhausted to deal with him today. Thankfully Larry had already approached him and was kindly directing Don and his bag pipe away. Good attorneys are like that- skillful in directing your boat away from the rocks. Still, Ben had to admit, most times, Don did keep life interesting even when you least expected it. This was not one of those times.

Order restored, they went back to the recitation of the Kaddish. After the solemn prayer, it was finally time to lay Ann to rest. The cemetery workers gently lowered the simple pine box into the ground. Then it was time for the mourner's starting with Ben first to start filling in the dirt. Ben did this by flipping the shovel upside down before shoveling the dirt in accordance with Jewish tradition. (It representing what an unnatural act of burying a loved one is.) After a couple of feeble shovelfuls, he passed the shovel to his daughter Esther who did the same. And that was it, his beloved, bubbly, intelligent, kind, loving wife was gone. Where did all of her go? Why did she have to go? God didn't answer and neither could Ben. He felt faint from emotion and needed to sit. His heartache sat down with him.

Chapter 1

The Current Beginning

Sometime later. It was Don's idea to take the trip and they had made the decision at the last minute but then Ben had the time. A lot of time. As a Union attorney, Ben believed in the power of democracy but democracy spit him out when the long term union president had been defeated in the union's local election. So at age 58, job over, wife gone, kids grown up, house paid off, Ben had time to putz about the country. IF- he really wanted to. It had been 14 months since Ann had been buried.

But Don, Ben's friend since Junior High, on the other hand, shouldn't have had so much time available. He'd been spending 50-60 hours a week on a special project he called: "Payback". That's how Don was, he ran all hot or cold and there didn't seem to be a medium setting. His wife, Deb, knew better than to try and adjust his settings. To entice Ben into going, Don was even willing to let Ben take his car the 2007 sweet ride Cadillac SRX chariot to seal the deal so Ben would come.

Ann, Ben's wife, really liked this last minute travel idea, thinking it would be good for Ben to get away for a while: "Come on, Ben, what have you got to lose? You got the time. Too much of it." She cooed: "It's been a tough year. I've been dead for over a year and all you do is sit in that Lazy Boy recliner and mope. You gonna spend the rest of your life, perfecting your sigh?" The men in Ben's family were really good at sighing. At family celebrations, they used to compete in competitive sighs when talking around a table about their daughter who had just gotten divorced or their son who had dropped out of college. Yet again. It was as if they were all trying out for part of Job the Prophet who had been tested with more tsuris (bad luck) than anyone had a right to deserve. Right now, Ben still believed he deserved a direct shot at the semifinals. Ann thought Ben was way overplaying his feeling sorry for himself. A lot.

In any case, Ben knew Ann was right and had his best interest at heart. (Almost always did.) He was lucky to have her now. Sort of. Yes, she was physically gone, but emotionally, she was still right there with him. Always had been. Before she died, she said she'd stay by his side. So she had. When she first appeared during the wee hours of the night, 4 months ago, Ben thought he had lost his mind. After his kids and sister forced him to, he even consulted a highly recommended (read expensive) psychiatrist who advised sleep aids and antidepressants. This made him even more groggy and no less depressed. So after thinking it over, he made the rational decision to dump the shrink and keep Ann. He felt better and no longer had a copay.

So there he was in the Caddy, early the next day, at Don's house which was the only house on the street with its lights on. Ben doubted that Don was up yet he knew better than to wake up his best friend on what almost seemed to be one of their silly high school high pranks. True, it was only 4:30 am but Don had originally wanted to leave even earlier. Yet Don was simply another eternal optimist who chronically overslept his appointments. Ben rejected Don's initial suggested departure time, pointing out that Bars closed at 2:30 am and drunk drivers would likely be still looking for sober cars to hit. Of course, Don wasn't ready to go even now later, so Ben waited quietly o Don's house.

It was beyond dark outside, it felt like a thick, black soup to Ben. Dark. Wanting to sleep. Waiting. Even a little foreboding. He must have dozed off because the next thing he knew, Don was standing next to him holding what looked like a Halloween bag full of Twinkies, Ho-Hos, licorice and who knows what. Only Don knew for sure and he probably threw in several strips of stale beef jerky for nutritional value. Like many men, Don firmly believed in the power of decayed animal flesh. Ben wondered if he should put his dentist on speed dial if they both were going to pretend, not only their bodies, but their teeth were 30 years younger and stronger too. Ben was beginning to think that this road trip was a stupid idea, no matter what Don or Ann said.

"Ben? Are you listening? I got treats, lots of them. If we stop for coffee at Brad's Gas, we can hop on Hwy 494 and miss most of the construction on Highway I-35 going south. My treat...This is gonna be great! Just as good as our old road trips." Don was talking faster and his voice was getting higher. Like he was on helium. He was excited. This was not good because the only thing worse than an excited Don was a depressed Don. Still, Don seemed to really need this trip when he called Ben the night before last and Ann reminded Ben that he still owed Don for really being there after all those dark days after Ann died.

It had happened so quickly. One day, Ann was a bubbly, loving, full of energy partner, soon to be retired and free. Several days later, she was dead from a series of strokes. It had started with a series of blinding headaches that no amount of Tylenol was ever going to fix. They had quickly doctored, then hospitalized Ann quickly and even tried that miracle stroke TPA drug. (Meaning Tissue Plasminogen Activator or TPA) But there just wasn't enough time and the TPA medication was administered too late. (Anything over 4 hours after the stroke is typically not as effective) All too soon his precious Ann was gone. Life wasn't supposed to turn out that way. But sometimes it did. Looking back now, Ben thought that time in the emergency room felt like a 2 hour Hallmark movie being played at too high a rate of speed. For months, Ben replayed that movie, over and over again- thinking what could he have done differently or if only he had recognized the beginning signs of Ann's stroke.

But that wasn't going to change anything now so Ben sighed inside where no one could hear and sucked it up for his high school audience of one:

"Sure, Don.. Sounds great. Let's stop at Brad's and then we can start grooving and moving forward on the interstate."

Ben pretended to throw out his imaginary cigarette and hoped Ann was right.

Brad's Auto World and Gas Emporium was an over the top extravaganza, full of gas, treats, 12 kinds of coffee, and occasionally clean restrooms. It was bright, it was large and it even had a white fiberglass hot rod 1948 Chevy rotating on the roof. It was simply too much, and exactly what they needed before leaving on their voyage of self-discovery. By the time Ben left the restroom, Don had already selected a twelve pack of Twinkies, even more beef jerky, and a Rand McNally Map of The United States (Interstate Edition). At only $7.95, the map made the trip feel more real and they hadn't even left the parking lot. The map was a symbol of a bygone era where people made their important decisions-relying on paper: newspapers, magazines, encyclopedias, now people just pushed a couple computer keys and electrons delivered their answers instantaneously. Ben was worried that in a decade or two, students wouldn't even know how to open a book. He smiled as he remembered the time Don and Ben had driven after finals to Florida. Don bet that they could make it with only a compass and no map. In the days before smart phones and Google, this escapade did not end well. Don refused to use any map on that trip- even when they had ended up in Alabama Gulf Coast. Since the Gulf of Mexico did encompass Florida, Don insisted he was not wrong but rather, just a bit more meandering. Whatever.

After fortifying themselves with Columbian Supreme Coffee and 13 gallons of gas, they were on their way. This time complete with a brand new map that would hopefully get them first to Austin, Texas where Ben's sister lived. Then by taking a right, ending up on West Interstate-10, it was only another 1,000 miles to Phoenix and finally a short 120 miles north up Highway I-17 to Sedona. This is where Ben and Ann had kept their winter home and where their Retiree Red Rock Dreams still resided. Ben hadn't been there in almost a year.

It was time to go back. Ben needed to sort out what to do about the home and his dreams. He was going to start having to make decisions starting with the Sedona winter house. The house was something that Ben wasn't sure he could still afford- financially or emotionally. Money was going to be more of an issue with Ann being gone. He was receiving the lessor survivor's pension and Ann's social security had ended. All in all, Ben was receiving $5000 less a month since Ann passed and he still had the same basic expenses ie the condo in Minneapolis, 2 cars(he'd sell Ann's but just hadn't had the heart to do it yet.) and the home in Sedona that had tripled in value since they bought it but still cost about $ 12,000 a year to carry. Still, Ben wasn't complaining he had more than most and the two of them had been pretty comfortable before Ann's death. Ben wasn't going to let himself make a decision without going to Arizona first. Ann had said what the wait was for, why not just go there and make up your mind? She was annoyed by Ben's indecisiveness since she died.

Ben used to be so confident. What attorney and especially litigator, isn't? But now, Ben found it hard to make decisions. Life was so uncertain now. Yes, it was long past time since he had gone out to Sedona. Yes, he did need to make a decision on what to do with the house. Of course, Ben knew this- with or without Ann. It felt easier to make no decision than the wrong decision. So that's what Ben did- pretty much nothing since Ann died. Though right now it did feel good to be on the road even if it wasn't 5 am yet. Ben was moving. He was doing something.

After an hour on I-35, after chewing on the thought for a while, Ben asked Don why he was so eager to get out of town. Don squinted, glanced in the rear view mirror, saw nothing of course and then finally explained:

"I was worried about you. Ann's been gone for over a year and you've been just camped out on your couch and Lazy Boy. You haven't been sleeping or eating and it's almost as if you're shrinking away, in front of all of us. I just thought an adventure trip might wake you up. "

Ben looked up in the rearview mirror and saw Ann was listening just like old times, her chin resting on both hands, so Ben decided to go easy on his friend:

"Well, Don, I appreciate your concern but this trip sure came up in a hurry. How are things going at work?"

Even at the best of economic times, work was a sensitive subject for Don. He was a brilliant computer nerd when it came to computer programming, but not so great when it came to dealing with people. Don worked best when he worked alone or from home on sophisticated, complex projects.

Don looked at his fingernails, decided they wouldn't give an answer and then said: "Funny, you should mention that. Things have been slow at work, so I offered to use my PTO to keep a full paycheck and they agreed to pick up the health insurance cost for 30 days."

"Does Deb know about this?" Ben answered his own question after watching Ann shake her head:

"Of course not, she was sleeping and now we're out of town. You better tell her." At times Don avoided difficult issues with his domestic supervisor. This was not wise. Don often claimed what Deb didn't know couldn't hurt him. That was not true. You always told your spouse what was or wasn't going on. Life was simpler that way and you maintained trust in your partner. Don's policy of escapade first, confession later was a significant strain on their marriage. Ben had been telling him that for years. Still, Ben did not remember signing up to be Don's relationship counselor. He must have been assigned in the snack aisle.

Deb was a Saint. Being married to Don and living through his shenanigans, she had to be.

"No reason for me to wake her up and upset her equilibrium if I'm back at work in 30 days. I left a note.. Besides, I am really worried about you,

| 17

the aspiring couch potato and I think this trip might help you harvest your crop."

"Might help, you but just leaving a note does not constitute understanding and a prior agreement. That was merely conflict avoidance on your part. I'm serious, guy, don't put off what you're going to regret for not saying, later. You have to talk to her!" Ben thought his logic made so much sense that maybe he could bill for being an attorney/therapist on this travel segment but instead Ann angrily POPPED off. Ben and Ann had this argument before about what tone Ben used when he "counseled" his best friend. When Ben talked this way, Ann felt he was reverting to his old blame and shame game. But he wasn't shaming Don if it was true. Ann often left when she got irritated with something Ben said, didn't really matter to her if it was true or not. A lot of times, it was more important to Ann how you said it, not just what you said. So in the good old days when she was physically here, she would walk out of the room, rather than say something that at least one of them would regret.

Now as a Spirit, she could pop in whenever she wanted but wouldn't stay when she was irritated. She called it a power surge- kinda like a Spirit having a migraine. Even after the 4 months Ben had been seeing her again, he found the POPPING in and out a little disconcerting so he did his best to try avoid alienating her. He wished he had done more of that when she was alive.

The miles passed. Ben saw first the cities of Faribault and then Owatonna in the rear mirror. Life was like that. People kept on driving towards something, and before they knew it, they had passed it. Even more so in the dark. Ben just kept his foot on the accelerator. Steady. No cruise control for this guy. His ankle could provide all the speed control he needed. Meanwhile, Don was still sleeping now in spite of the 4 Twinkies he had eaten so far on the trip.

It was now becoming sunrise. The red and orange were widening from a pencil thin view from the East. There is just those few minutes of sunrise before that orange orb becomes the blinding sun, so Ben decided to take advantage of the flat empty expanse of Iowa to try and take a photograph with his phone. Since no one else was awake, he thought he could accomplish it one handed while driving the car. Besides, he was driving on a separated highway. Still was not a good idea. His left hand had a difficult time focusing the shot while keeping the left side mirror out of the frame. When he almost dropped the phone, he overcompensated by swerving to the right. He regained control. Thankfully, no one was nearby and Don was still sleeping.

Don wondered what percentage of accidents were caused by middle aged men who were bored or unwilling to accept they no longer had the same eye-hand coordination that they did at age 30. After his most recent stunt, Ben was more than willing to accept his change of coordination status. Still felt pretty good to be moving about the country. About an hour later. Ann POPPED back in, she was over being angry:

"Miss me?"

Ben shushed her: "You gonna wake up Don!"

"Nope. Remember only you can see or hear me. But you could wake up Don with your strong masculine voice."

"No worries, I'll just use my soft, whiney, husband voice."

"HA."

"Good to see and hear you. Gosh, I miss you."

"What you really miss is actually sleeping with me."

"Well, our physical relationship did offer certain fringe benefits that I no longer have direct access to." Ben thought this sounded pretty sophisticated but Ann wasn't buying it:

"Is that all, you guys care about?"

"No, but it's important. It counts. It excites me. It calms me. It comforts me. I really, really do miss our touch. (Porn didn't cut it even when it was recommended to him by another widower who was excitedly waiting for virtual reality.) Hey, I did want to ask you, if you're a Spirit, why do you really need to wear outfits?"

"Silly man, of course not. But I wanted you to focus on our talks. The virtual reality we use is like those fake background shots you see in Zoom meetings. It seems that humans are freaked by Spirits without a physical manifestation and besides, this way, I get to finally wear whatever I want, whenever I want- No more worries about price or proper size."

"Huh, no laundry bills, either..."

"I thought I looked good in blue Oscar De La Renta."

"Got time for a couple more questions?"

"For you? Always."

They were almost at the Iowa border still on I-35 which they would take all the way to Austin, Texas .They had lots of time. Ben used to love the old driving trips with Ann, the longer the better.

The couple had found nothing was off the table for discussion when they were on road trips:

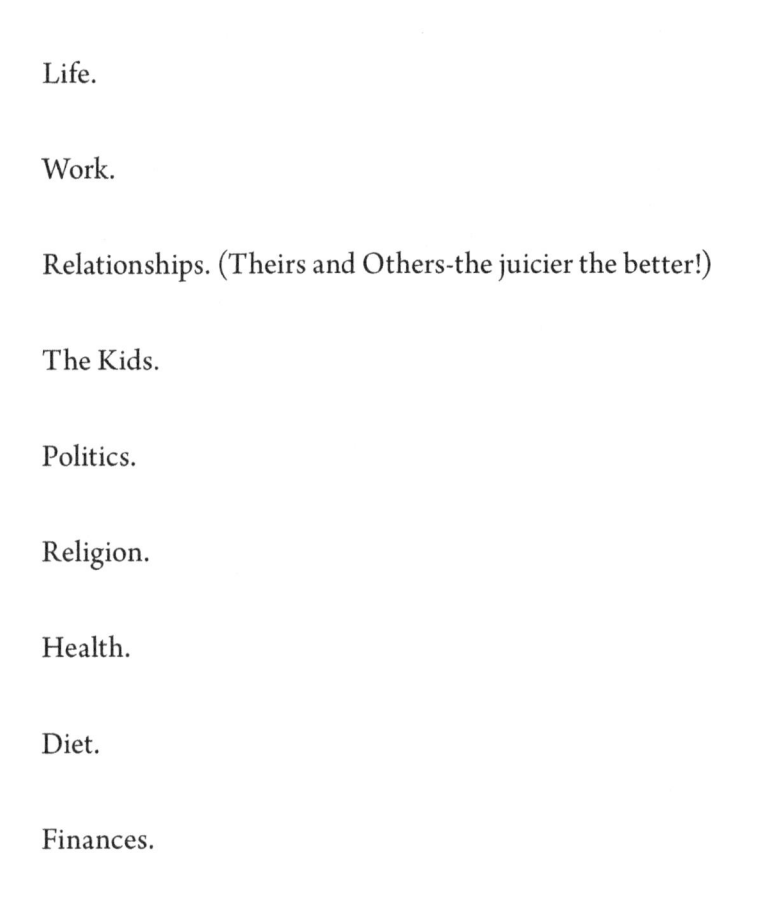

Life.

Work.

Relationships. (Theirs and Others-the juicier the better!)

The Kids.

Politics.

Religion.

Health.

Diet.

Finances.

When they were home, there was always a distraction or another room to flee to. Here on the long road, they managed to talk. On occasion, they even managed to listen to each other, respectfully.

Ben sighed, a gentle one: "I wish…anyways you could stick around all the time. Let me ask you this if you gave up the rental Del La Renta vision- could you linger around a little longer? Just to hear your voice is enough for me."

"Nah, from what I've been told by others hanging around the pool in the Cloud. It can't work that way. I'm almost out of my out juice and that's all I can use. Something about not overwhelming the polarity from inverting the Black Hole to borrow some time. Take too much and you go over the spending limit. I can only spend what I've saved in my own personal account."

"It sounds like overspending on a celestial debit card, how bout if I join up with you?"

Ann was not amused by this kind of talk:

"It doesn't work that way, there are no guarantees, that there is going to be an opening when you exit your body. Besides, the kids and grandkids want you, need you, right where you are. You should never joke about cashing in your life chips early"

"Sorry. I would just like a little more time with you." It reminded Ben of the days when they were dating and talking all the time, on the telephone. In those first few months of discovery, Ben would only hang up after Ann had disconnected. He didn't want to miss a single word. Ben still loved the soft caress of her voice. He still hated ending the connection first, even now.

"Tell you what, I will return the virtual gown early and gain some extra time credit tonight. How bout I just stay a spiritual voice with no virtual form, more, for the future? That could give me up to an extra hour for you each day.

Besides, my friend Sally wants the gown back anyways, for a Stephan King Horror dream she wants to implant on her third ex-husband."

Ann had talked to Ben about implanting thoughts before. She didn't believe in using it, even if it was for Ben's own good. People had to remember or learn things on their own. That's the type of person Ann was. Thoughtful and generous to a fault. But it wasn't a fault, it was just the way Ann was. No wonder she made the cut upstairs and became a free floating Spirit. Ben didn't seriously expect to even make through the interview process.

Just then, Don began to mumble and snort which both Ann and Ben knew from past experience meant he would be waking up soon. Ann sensed her energy level was wearing down and told Ben she would talk to him later. Even Spirits that had alternative energy systems occasionally needed to be replenished.

"Ahhhh," Don groaned: "I'm ready for breakfast. All those miles made me hungry." Don was always hungry. Always had been even when Ben had first met him. Don was a big man but wasn't fat, just solid. But as he aged, his metabolism slowed down and Don had to ride his bike 100 miles a week to stay in what he considered, his right shape. "How about a Maid Rite sloppy hamburger in Mason City?"

"Please don't." Maid Rite was an early sloppy hamburger chain that barely was hanging on in the Upper Midwest. Don had discovered it during one of their drunken tours of St. Cloud, Minnesota during college. Apparently because, sometimes things were not apparent to anyone but Don, since there was one Maid Rite in Mason City, Iowa, it was necessary to immediately conduct a memory taste test then and there. It still wasn't clear how many

Maid Rites remained or why. Maid Rite burgers were an acquired taste and like some people, Ben had never acquired it. Don, of course, had. He believed vitamin B (BBQ and Beef) was all a person needed for proper nutrition. Ben was still too reliant on microwaved meals although he was beginning to make his peace with fresh vegetables. Ben looked and saw that Des Moines was only another 120 miles further south.

"Tell you what, if we keep going straight to Des Moines, Iowa we can stop for an early lunch at the Embers around 10 am." Ben, a veteran of many trips with Don, had done some minimal advance research before the trip to avoid a Maid Rite made wrong for him.

Embers had been a larger Midwest (100 plus Restaurants) 24 hour burger/breakfast chain with the slogan of "Remember the Embers". Their specialty was the Emberger Royale which was a large beef patty covered with a raw onion, special seasoning and just enough bacon and cheddar cheese to put available cardiologists on standby alert. Overrun by the invasion of large casual restaurant chains like Panera, Applebee's, Ruby Tuesday and the like after the late 70's, there were still several rebel Ember restaurants with their distinctive roofs holding out in the Midwest. At least he hoped there were.

Every year, Don, Ben and their high school cronies made a pilgrimage to Rick's Embers in Fridley, Minnesota. The restaurant was there with all the old standbys and the largest collection of Embers' memorabilia in the galaxy though Ricky's Embers in Fridley, Minnesota was a close second. There, they feasted on well done Embergers, thick milk shakes and memories of high school times. Recently, Rick's announced that they were closing down and being repurposed into multi-unit housing. It was amazing how quickly favorite restaurants and stores became past tense. So there was no way Don was going to turn down this offer. It would still only be 10 am but Ben, at least, could get some breakfast with his coffee. He could really go for some of their blueberry pancakes.

So they continued to drive on the highway and Don checking his phone found out the Embers still existed at the junction of I-80 and Highway 59. The sky was by now, a steel grey without a cloud. Cold weather was on the way. It was late October and November winds were already calling early. Ben didn't blame the clouds for not coming out. It was too dang cold and dreary.

They both zipped their winter jackets and accepted the cold. Heck, they were from Minnesota and that's what Minnesotans do- they accept the cold, not embrace it. Don't have to like it but you learn to deal with it. They walked in the Embers and they were back in the 80's. Booth seating everywhere, except in front of the kitchen where there still was a white Formica counter with bar stools. They still had the 12 page menu and it was a perfect stop for a long road trip. Build the base with basics, Don always used to say. Don also used to say that a full stomach led to full comprehension but Ben didn't understand whether it was true or what it even meant. Ben had the blueberry pancakes which he hoped would sop up all the strong coffee swirling around unhappily in his stomach.

There was no question what Don was going to have: an Emberger Royale (Well done, of course.) with a Banana Shake. Not many places served that flavor of shake anymore. As a meatarian, that is, a former vegetarian until the ripe old age of 22, He had been overcompensating since college. Don had never met a burger he couldn't devour, no matter what time it was. 2 am, 6 am, 3 pm, 11 pm, it didn't matter. Don called it his never ending, always satisfying, protein diet and Don said he couldn't wait until they got into beef bbq country, ie somewhere at or south of Kansas City. Ben made a mental note to himself to make sure he didn't forget his Lipitor. He didn't want to meet his maker too soon.

Breakfast was great just as their stomachs remembered. Ben relented, and ordered the Banana Cream pie, a specialty to accompany his necessary coffee. At 1200 calories and piled high with banana slices topped with over an inch of whipped cream, The Banana Crème Pie alone was almost worth the drive. It was amazing to Ben to see what long term memories their stomachs had and what lengths people would go to feed them. Then it was back into their chariot, Ben's grey, slightly dented, silver 2007 Cadillac SRX with its exclusive, massive moon roof. Ben loved that car even now with 132,248 quality miles on it. He and Ann had made many trips to their winter home in it. With the moon roof exposed, almost all the way to the third row of seats, on clear nights, they could feel the moon glow upon them. Too many happy memories to ever let this automotive baby go. Even with Ann gone. No way.

Chapter 2

A Break in the Action

Back on I-35 on the way still to Kansas City, Ben felt Don was more likely to be honest, as a result of being sleepy and full of endorphins from the carbs and pie. Ben still wanted to know as to why Don took this leave and trip so suddenly: "Don, you awake or are you still napping?"

"That's a big 10-4, I am almost awake and at your disposal. I think that last Twinkie after our pre-lunch may have done me in. But give me time, I will recover. How about lunch in half an hour?"

"No you don't- before we left- you agreed that there would be at least a 3 hour delay between meals. This was an early lunch."

"But we never had breakfast!"

"What do you call what we just had at Embers?"

"That was snack. Even the cheap nursery school we went to gave morning snacks."

If it wasn't clear by now, Ben and Don went a long way back. Way back. Even before High School which is when they usually told people they had met. But nursery school taught them many lessons. But health or welfare or logic had no meaning for someone whose value system had been established by Mrs. Feldman in Room 5 when they were 4 years old.

"Too bad, I've got the wheel."

"Not for long!" and with that, Don lunged for the wheel. The never ending high school grudge match continued.

Even a Cadillac, whose target market appeared to be a 77 year old male, was not designed to accommodate two 60 year- 5 year olds fighting for control of the toy, ie the steering wheel of a 4000 lbs. automotive weapon, currently swerving on a major freeway.

"Let go before you kill someone!" Ben yelled.

"You let go first!" Don responded. There was a reason that after the first couple's adventure trip, both Deb and Ann had the good sense to always stay behind.

"That's crazy, then no one would be driving." Ben prided himself on being reasonable and logical.

"Why? You chicken? You gonna flinch, huh?" Don had a sick smile on his face. He knew how much Ben hated being challenged, going back to preschool.

So Ben did what they taught him to do in the Offensive Self Defense Course: He waited until Don leaned closer and used his right elbow as a battering ram, intent on breaking Don's nose. Chop. Chop. CRACK! That did not sound good and it wasn't. Ben knew he cracked something but since he was driving wasn't exactly sure what it is was. Ben hoped it wasn't something necessary.

Don let go of the steering wheel, moaned, and cupped his nose with both hands: "I think you broke my nose".

"I'll buy you a new one if you need it. You could have killed us or others out there, if I didn't stop you.. It was legitimate self-defense."

There was now a small river of bright, red blood now pouring out of Don's nose:

"Don, there's a box of Kleenex in the glove box. Help yourself."

Don grabbed the Kleenex and stuffed it up both nostrils: "You sure didn't."

"I'm sorry." Ben said. "I'll stop at an urgent care or emergency room if you want in Kansas City. Can you still breathe through your nose?"

Don tried to breathe through his nose without much success. He looked pitiful. The problem with trying to relive your high school adventures is the increasing toll that they take. Ben felt guilty as he often did, at the end of adventures with Don:

"Don, let's stop at an urgent care center in the northern suburbs of Kansas City. I'll even cover the copay. It's only an hour or two away." Ben wasn't sure how bad it was, though it looked like Don's nose had taken a slight right turn, courtesy of Ben. Kinda distinguished in a Sean Penn (the Actor) sort of way.

After a requisite amount of silent pouting, Don mumbled his agreement. Then he went back to silently looking at everything but Ben. This part of Iowa was sure boring. Only crops and cows once they were 15 minutes south of downtown Des Moines.

Before they knew it, they had crossed the border and were in Missouri. The topography still wasn't much to write home about, not that anyone did that anymore. Don was still pretty quiet. Still stewing. Ben had not forgotten about getting to the bottom of Don's haste to hit the road, but he decided to cut him some slack because of the nasal situation. Ben had to admit his defense instructor was right: elbows could be pretty lethal in certain situations if you knew how to use them. The real issue is to determine when to use these alleged "defensive" skills. Don, Ben was sure, would have argued that Ben's use was offensive. But Don wasn't talking.

Ben turned on the radio and found a FM station playing some golden oldies from the 70's and 80's. About 2 hours later, they saw a giant billboard advertising an urgent care clinic, 2 exits away. Since it was now already 3 pm, they decided to go to it.

The urgent care or urgency as they called it, was located in a non-descript office park that could have been located anywhere in America and probably was. Apparently, society declared its social advancement by repeatedly cloning ugly 3 story white office buildings surrounded by massive pads of free asphalt parking that together declared they had no soul.

They could have walked in together but they choose to come in separately. Don picked a corner far away from the 2 types of people that had come in for URGENT medical attention. The first group were suburban moms who brought their pint sized petri dishes (read children who had a cold). The second group were men, 50 or above, who had toughed out their illness or injury until they or their significant other couldn't take it anymore. Ben decided by default, that they fell into the second group. Ben then sat by himself in the opposite corner.

After Don filled out the required paperwork, they waited well over an hour for Don to get called. Apparently Urgency was not the same as Emergency. Urgency referred to how quickly they ran your credit card. Ben did offer to pay as long as they would accept his Delta card so he at least got the points out of the mishap but Don said he only let true friends pay for his nose. Then Ben asked if he should come in also but Don responded that Ben had already done, more than enough, thank you very much. It was the longest verbal interaction they had, since the nasal remodeling, now several hours ago.

Ben waited in his obscure non-descript corner. Luckily, he still had his public library eBooks loaded on his phone. For some reason, Ben thought Call of the Wild by Jack London was an appropriate choice.

The time passed, not quickly, but with a warning from Jack London how Nature was not to be denied. There was a useful lesson in there, but Ben was too tired to figure out what it was. He had now been up over 16 straight hours and he hopefully still had a date tonight with Ann. He was getting older and he could barely handle half of an exam prep all nighter that he used to handle, without a second thought, in college, many years ago. Maybe all three of them could spend the night in Kansas City.

After another hour, Don came out wearing a taped white cross on his nose. Ben wondered if it was necessary or if Don was warning Ben to leave him alone. It wasn't. Ben had broken Don's nose and they had to reset it. Luckily, the doctor who set it was also an amateur hockey player and had reset many noses without general anesthetics over the years. Don didn't feel so lucky. It still hurt. A lot. Don was still pissed at Ben and was still trying to limit himself to one syllable words at first in response to questions except when he couldn't help himself. Don was also on some strong Ibuprofen pain medication.

"Thanks a lot, Ben, You broke my nose and now my nose looks like the Messiah on the Cross. I gotta wear this for 8 to 10 weeks until the bones set. Jesus Christ, what were you thinking?"

"I was thinking you grabbing the steering wheel could have been our final thrill ride. I'm sorry, I really am that I broke your nose. How about I treat you to some real Kansas City BBQ in Kansas City, you pick- my treat again?"

"Again? There's no way you're getting within 3 yards of my nose. Don't think, you buying my nose, BBQ lets you off the hook."

Still, real Kansas City BBQ was an attractive offer to Don even if he could no longer really smell it. Don had earlier explained that the difference between Kansas City BBQ (Pork ribs) and Texas BBQ (Beef ribs) was greater than the type of mammal one devoured. There was the sauce (KC, lots of it) and no sauce Texas. (Dry rubbed spices only)

Don already knew where he wanted to go: "Ok, let's go to Slap's. You can get the sliced beef brisket and I can try the potato salad, pork ribs, burnt ends and turkey." So off they went.

It was that good. Fans would wait over 2 hours for their ribs. Ben tried talking him into Jack Stack BBQ which had a number of more convenient locations in the area but there was no changing the heart of a true BBQ zealot. The opportunity of having BBQ at least once a day and hopefully twice, made the whole trip very desirable to Don. Right now Ben wanted to keep Don happy and he wondered for a second, if his homeowner's umbrella policy would cover something like this. Nah, Don would never sue him, he just wasn't that type of guy, Ben decided. He was wrong. Don was that type of guy:

"You know, I might sue over, on how you redeveloped my nose. I feel like you just added a 3 story parking ramp on the inside of my nose. I hope you got all kinds of really good insurance. You're gonna need it by the time my attorneys are done with you. Did I mention, the intentional infliction of emotional distress?"

"Oh please, put a cork in it. Friends don't sue friends."

"Well, former friends do.."

Ben stared ahead and drove. Ben had been looking forward to getting to Kansas City and by that he meant Kansas City, Missouri, which was by far, larger than Kansas City, Kansas. Population wise, Kansas City, Kansas was even smaller than Overland Park, Kansas. (Yes, the similar names confused a lot of people)

Kansas City, Mo had the largest number of fountains in the world after Rome (over 200) and impressive memorials to the Great War. In those days, they believed that there wouldn't be more than one. (i.e. WW1).

But Ben and Don were both hurting. Don more so, but Ben was still tired. Ben, as driver, brought up the current travel facts of life: "Look we have 3 more hours to Wichita and then it's still 8 hours further to Austin. How about we spend the night here and power through all the way to Austin in one day?"

"How long of a drive will that be?" Don, under pain, asked a reasonable question.

"Nothing we haven't done before-750 miles. We can do it easy if we are on the road by 7 am." Ben listened to himself and thought it sounded doable.

Don thought it over: "Ok, as long as I can have BBQ for Breakfast. I don't care where we stay." Don always had his personal priorities in order. Next he closed his eyes and felt the pain.

Ben looked around and saw a Hampton Inn across the road. Good enough. Ben drove there. No question that they were getting 2 separate rooms after the day they had. "See you at 7 am." Ben said. Don grunted an affirmative response. They each went to sleep, again in their separate corners.

CHAPTER 3

SOMETIMES, A HOT SHOWER IS NOT ENOUGH.

Ben walked into the highly rated sterile motel room with his bags. There were white vanilla walls, a king sized bed on one side and dark wood like furniture on the other wall. It had been a long day. Getting up at 3:30 am, Don's insistence on getting out of Minneapolis, driving hundreds of miles, the struggle over the steering wheel, breaking Don's nose, waiting for hours at the Urgency- Ben thought they had done more than enough for one day, they still had 750 miles tomorrow before they got to his sister's. Yep, it sure had turned into a fun adventure trip. He hadn't heard from Ann so he decided to take a shower and just climb into bed. Ben wasn't sure if Spirits could smell, but he sure could. Ben knew he needed it. He took a really long, hot shower and it seemed to wash off some of the mileage.

But as he dried himself off and looked into the steamed mirror, he saw a simple message written into the steam: Hi there, Mr. Good Looking. He smiled when he recognized Ann's handiwork and called out to her: "Ann? Are you there?"

Thankfully she was: "Boy, I know 2 guys or should I say boys who had a really tough day."

"Gosh, it's such a relief to be able to talk to you after a day like today."

"Yeah, I heard." According to Ann, listening did not take up much energy.

"He could've killed both of us with his stunt. I don't know what's going on with him, but there's something really wrong. More than usual."

"Cut him some slack. He's off work and you just multiplied the number of noses he has." Ann was a kind, gentle person who didn't believe in the use of physical force. Besides she had always been fond of Don. Some of Ben's earlier girlfriends hadn't and Don was a deal maker or breaker, depending on a person's point of view. Ann understood Don. Not everybody did.

"Having one nose isn't all it's cracked up to be." Ben thought it was pretty clever.

Ann didn't: "Neither is your sense of humor. You know this could affect his asthma this winter."

"I already apologized and covered the copay. (Don had finally relented and let Ben pay him back.) I even bought him dinner. What else can I do?"

"Besides promising not to turn him into mashed potatoes, you can listen to him when he wants to talk. You're right of course, there is something very wrong going on." Even before Ann died, she had always been a sympathetic listener to Don. He sure needed it.

"Ok, I promise. Wanna listen to some TV?"

"Look you have a long drive tomorrow. Why don't we turn off the lights and talk for a while?"

They both loved talking in the dark to each other in bed. In some ways it felt more intimate than even being able to see each other. They never ran out of things to discuss and almost never went to bed angry with each other. Before Ann came back, this is what Ben truly missed the most. These simple conversations in the dark.

"Sounds good to me. How was your day?"

"Not bad, no complaints." Ann had never been one of those people who when asked how their day was going, answered: hanging in there or just getting by in the hopes, they would get to, once again, go through their never ending list of complaints.

"So what did you do all day?" Ben was curious. When she and her body were both around, she liked to discuss both their day especially when they had happy hour.. Now she usually didn't say much, maybe she had signed a no discussion clause as part of her Spirit employment compensation package.

"Not much. The usual."

"Well, that's illuminating." Ben switched off the light.

"Don't go snarky on me. I went to the ends of the universe to get enough energy to spend the night here."

"You'll be here all night? That's grand." Ben loved going to sleep and waking up next to Ann. It was the last thing he heard at night and the first voice he listened to in the morning. It made it seem like old times. Well, it wasn't exactly the same but it sure beat staying up at night alone watching a bunch of old videos or not having her by him. In a weird way, they were still together. Sort of. Ben knew he was lucky to have, whatever he had, of her.

Ben was getting tired. He yawned, then asked: "So what do you think happened to Don and why is he running?"

"Do you think he got the ax at work? If you want I can have one of my friends in the cloud, get ahold of his personnel records."

"Nah, I think your original advice was better. I'll wait him out and listen to what he says. "

Ben adjusted his pillow and turned on his side: "Good night sweet pea, love you honey. You got enough juice to hang around and wake me at 6 am with a rainbow?" Ben loved the special effects Ann could pull off when she had enough juice. Besides, he hated waking up in what was now usually, an empty room.

"I'll do my best."

Ben had one more thought: "You still think I shouldn't try to explain what we've got going on again to the kids or my sister Fran?"

"You know what happened last time when you tried to explain,,, you ended up, not by choice, against your will, at the psychiatrist and on medication."

"I know. But people have a hard time accepting what they can't see or understand."

"Exactly. I know they love you and mean well but their fear won out. Let's get through this trip and then revisit it later."

"You know best."

"I'm glad you finally, recognize that. Now go to sleep honey and we will talk in the morning. I'll stick around til you are sleeping."

Ben sighed contentedly, couldn't keep his heavy eyelids open any longer and promptly fell asleep. As usual. Someone had to be the Scout for Dreamland.

CHAPTER 4

TEXAS HOLD IT

6 am came with a kaleidoscope of color. It was as if he woke up during a dream, when he was 10 years old and had been back at the State Fair with cotton candy and a rainbow mixed in. He liked going there, a lot. WOW, again as usual. It didn't matter if it was a dream or real, he just liked being at the State of Minnesota's finest and most fattening tradition. Then Ben fully opened his eyes and he was back in the Kansas City Hampton Inn. While that was a disappointment, just hearing Ann's voice almost made up for it:

"Ben, time to get up! You've got a very long day ahead of you."

Ben still loved the sound of Ann's voice. It reminded him of how lucky they were to have whatever they had now. He would never take it for granted. He never had. When Ann was alive, he liked to bring her coffee every morning and use that as an excuse to bring up how he felt about their issues. Even though as a guy, he didn't like to talk about issues especially feelings so early in the day, he was getting better at talking them out and - even more importantly, listening to what Ann thought. That in turn showed Ann that he valued her feelings and respected her judgment especially with the passage of time. That joint partnership continued to this day. Death did not end it. Most men needed constant and consistent educational reinforcement on both talking and feelings. Ben, to his credit, not as much.

"Hey, thanks for the wakeup! That color parade at the Fair, it was fabulous! How was your night?" Ben still wasn't sure if Spirits slept, he had a lot to learn about his wife, even after 31 years.

"It was fine- like a soft rain." Even if Ben couldn't see it, he felt a gentle smile.

"How about you, Ann, you got a ticket to ride with us today?"

"Wish I could but I used it all up with the color extravaganza. I gotta head back and charge up. I'll see you at Fran's around 8 pm. Love ya". Ann made a POPPING sound and she was gone. Ben decided to grab some oatmeal and coffee at the free buffet downstairs. His stomach couldn't stomach more BBQ, this early in the morning. He bet Don could. Ben actually felt pretty good. He slept well with Ann nearby and got up to pee at night, only once.

Outside, Don was already waiting and was wearing a western shirt with white snap buttons, cowboy boots, cowboy hat and even a bolo. Don looked like he belonged on a PBS Kids Show. Oh God, this was too much especially at 7 am, thought Ben. Then he smiled as he thought how Don had dressed for the last Vegas trip. At least, this time, he was not wearing a reflective silver suit and pinky ring.

Ben, on the other hand, was dressed in his usual University of Minnesota hoodie and blue jeans. At least the hoodie wasn't inside out. It had happened before. Ben, as Ann liked to say: "had a low clothing IQ.."

He just didn't care about how he was dressed. Inside out, outside in, mismatched socks, tucked in, tucked out, labels showing, it didn't matter to Ben as long as his clothes were clean. What really mattered was what you wore on the inside, not what you wore on the outside. Things had only gotten worse since Ann died and there was no one anyone anymore to advise him when he had gotten it wrong, yet again. Don's wife had once accused him of ghost writing the book: Dress for Disgust.

But there they were at 7 am, looking for BBQ. Seriously. Don said you never knew when the Good Lord would take you so you had to go for all the BBQ you could whenever you could. Strangely enough, Don found what he hoped smelled like adequate BBQ at the gas station they stopped at to gas up the car. Though with his reupholstered nose, Don could not be sure. But he went ahead and bought 3 burnt end tacos even though he didn't know how long the tacos had been out there or where the BBQ burnt ends came from.. Don believed just like in life, sometimes you had to take a risk and that included gas station prepared food.

So they were off and only 743 miles to go before they were done for the day. Don and Ben had put a lot of miles on together since their teens. There was the infamous (at least to them) 24 hour marathon straight without stopping to New York City and several trips to Florida. Then, there were the trips to California and the national parks on the way. There was a comfort in a shared history among friends, even if Don was more than satisfied by his burnt ends, and he slept through the morning miles as they floated on I-35.

But Ben didn't feel sleepy at all. Instead he spent the miles, trying to recall every person by class year who went to high school with him. So long ago. At times, he remembered faces but not names. At others, he could see their names but not the faces. He was pleased to know he could still attach a majority of the names and faces. He wondered what they looked like now. He wondered if they wondered how HE looked now, though Facebook, kept one as informed and sometimes more than informed, as they wanted to be.

The miles dragged on. Don was still sleeping and Ben hadn't heard from Ann since the morning wakeup. He wished he had more of a regular schedule with Ann but maybe this kept their relationship fresher. Or maybe she had a mandatory SECC or Spiritual Education Credit Class on a variety of topics. From the little, Ann had talked about it, the courses ranged from when the best time was to implant dreams to stiffening the emotional spine.

But regardless, the next time they talked, he was going to pin her down to a regular visiting schedule, although that might prove difficult with a Spirit that had no physical form. The silver Caddy cocoon continued speeding down the road. Finally, in frustration, he turned on the radio and found some country western. He turned the volume up LOUD to get Sleeping Beauty's attention. Don may have loved dressing like a cowboy still couldn't handle country western. No way.

The slumbering giant in the front seat began to wake: "Turn that damn thing off!" Don believed that too high a dose of country western music could affect your IQ.

Then seconds later, "Where the heck are we?"

"Somewhere near Oklahoma City, Oklahoma."

"How far have we gone?"

"About 350 miles since breakfast, about 400 miles still to go."

"Wow, you're making good time."

"Right now it's time for lunch. We're running low on gas and I need to pee anyway. My bladder is about to quit."

"What time is it?"

"Can't your stomach still tell time?"

Don glanced at his watch. It was close to 12 pm. As males over the age of 50, they were both part of the declining group that still wore watches. Their kids no longer did. No need. Like everyone else, the kids relied on their phones for the time, weather, news, social media and just basically all the information available not just on the planet but the universe.

"We're making good headway on the miles."

Don checked his phone: "The closest good BBQ is Ralph's Smokehouse. (Don had a special App: BBQ or Else.) It's right off I-35 and they have fast take out. Reviews say that they have the best fried okra and beef brisket around."

"How far away?" Someone had to keep this tour on time.

"About 30 minutes." Don was willing to wait for real good BBQ. It was that important to him.

"Deal as long as we get it take out. I'll have the beef brisket sandwich with a Dr. Pepper soda."

Real Dr. Pepper was big in Oklahoma and Texas. Some people in Oklahoma and Texas even drank it for breakfast. Dr. Pepper was invented in Waco, Texas and claimed to be the oldest continually produced soda in the US going back to 1885. (In case you're interested Coca Cola came along in 1886

But Don had more important things to think about: "I'll have the beef\ pork rib, dry rubbed combo, with the fried okra. Probably with a diet Dr. Pepper." There Don was being diet conscious, though with the amount of salt and sugar in his diet, why bother? His pancreas had surrendered a long time ago and Don now took daily medication for his diabetes.

Don was a fanatic on BBQ but was willing to defer his typical diet coke to follow the taste dictates of the local population. As a person who loved to travel, instead of buying postcards to remember a trip, Don permanently "borrowed" restaurant menus. This trip was going to significantly add to his collection. Don advised Ben that someday restaurants would no longer offer paper menus and that customers would rely instead on scanning the menus on their smart phones. Never happen, Ben thought. Already was.

"Ok, I'll get the gas after." Ben was still trying to be agreeable. Ralph's was on a side street in a residential neighborhood. It was further than Ben wanted to go, but he figured he could stop for gas after for far less than interstate prices. The Caddy was thirsty and did drink a lot of gas.

Ralph's was a converted grey rambler home that had picnic tables in the front with parking and 3 BBQ smokers in the back. One could smell Ralph's long before they actually got there. Apparently the business had started in Ralph's garage and neighbors didn't mind. People therein, the City, had the freedom not to have any city zoning and each Thanksgiving, Ralph threw a free neighbors only, smoked turkey and ham meal to keep relations friendly.

They both accepted the free plastic bibs with Ralph's motto on them:" Ralph's BBQ: Finger Licking, Lip Smacking Good! "

Don and Ben also took plenty of the free paper towels and handy wipes. The BBQ was as good as promised. Don had ordered the spicy dry rub and it left a slight pepper burn on his lips. It also left a pleasurable mesquite smoke sensation in his nose which could thankfully, now smell. Don cheated and also had several extra containers of different sauces with his combo. For True Texas BBQ, sauces were supposed to be unnecessary, especially if there was a competent dry rub, but even Don the Purist, could not resist. His favorite was the Devil's Daily Revenge. Don thought the beef ribs were better than the pork but felt he had erred by ordering the fried okra over the homemade pepper coleslaw.

Then they stopped at a local gas chain On Cue that had cleaner bathrooms than Ben had seen in some doctor's offices and Don enjoyed their Wide World of Jerky. He topped off his meal with Bison and Goose Jerky for dessert.

It was therefore no surprise when Don quickly fell into a protein based induced sleep stupor shortly outside of Pauls Valley, Oklahoma, home of the Toy and Action Figure Museum. According to the Road Sign, it had the world's largest collection of action figures with everything from the Robot on Lost in Space to GI Joe to R2D2 from Star Wars. The sign advised it had a large collection of comics and dress up costumes. Ben could not decide if he was disappointed or relieved that Don had slept through the exit for

Don would have insisted on stopping. He had dodged a sartorial bullet for Don would have played with the costumes for hours. Ben shuddered as he pictured Don at the Ann's funeral in his Scottish motif. No, Ben wanted to keep on moving. Austin was now less than 350 miles away and Dallas Fort Worth was only a 150 miles down the road.

So with Ben asleep and no word from Ann, Ben just kept on driving. Like a lot of guys, he found long distance driving the endless flat prairie or for that matter, anywhere relaxing. He didn't really understand why, but maybe it was because it was a relatively mindless goal with a purpose. Or maybe, thought Ben, it was the other way around- it was a mindless purpose with a goal. Either way, Ben was enjoying the ride, even by himself. He could think about things, deep things, even if he wasn't sure, what they all were while he was driving. It almost felt like the slight buzz, he got from 2 or 3 beers sitting outside on a nice summer eve. Automotive meditation he called it when he once tried to explain the feeling he got driving to Ann.

They had just passed into Texas and were approaching Denton. Interstate Highway 35 split into 2 routes I-35E which went to Dallas and I-35 W that ran through Fort Worth. Both Roads merged back into I-35 near Hillsboro. With no one to disagree, Ben decided to go through the more truly Texan city of Fort Worth. It was only 40 to 45 miles to Fort Worth. Plus his high school friends Bill and Sally lived there. Maybe he should at least just call them. Maybe even see them. Either way, then it was a cake walk to Austin less than 200 miles and he even got to drive through Waco. Ben was going to have to spend some time on a future trip to Fort Worth. He and Ann had always talked about going there for the true Texan Town that included a world class art museum. Residents of Fort Worth bragged their city had Sass and Class.

CHAPTER 5

DEEP IN THE HEART OF TEXAS

Suddenly, though Ben was no longer alone: "Hey there trucker, miss me?"

"Hey, I've been wondering where you were. It's good to hear your voice."

"Same here, I got charged up and wanted to spend some quality time with you before you got to Austin."

"Well, looks like you'll have plenty of time if Don doesn't wake up. Its only 12:30 pm and it's already rush hour traffic. I thought we had avoided that by going through Fort Worth instead of Dallas."

"Oh, stop your belly aching. Or maybe that's due to your 3rd or 4th round of BBQ. Hope you are at least remembering to take your cholesterol statins."

"I'll have you know that it's only my second in.."

Ann interrupted: "Less than 24 hours. Seriously, you've gotta do a better job of taking care of yourself now that I'm not here, all the time, to keep an eye on you."

"I'm working on it."

"Oh, stop talking like a teenager and their homework assignments. I really wanted to talk to you about the "Talk" you're going to have with your sister Fran. You know she's going to ask about us.."

Ann loved Fran but was now wary around her sister in law and she had good reason to be. Fran was a "2fer"-Sissy was both an older sister and a social worker. This meant she knew what was best for people on both a professional AND personal basis. As a professional, Fran advised them what they could do. Yet an older sister, Sissy told Ben often what he should do. And Ben knew what Fran would say as a sister, if she found out that Ben and Ann had gotten back together again. Sort of. Still, Fran had a heart of gold that shone fiercely bright.

Ben let Ann's words hang for a minute. Then he spoke:

"I know why you're concerned and I don't blame you. I remember how upset Fran and the kids got when I tried to explain how we had gotten back in touch the first time. I tried to explain how many widows and widowers talked to their dead spouses. You just started to answer me back."

" You know what's going to happen. She's gonna ask and I know what you're gonna tell her. The truth, as we see it. Then her next calls are going to be to our kids and the 4th will be to the psychiatrist. Is that what you really want?"

"Well, no but I don't want to keep it a secret any longer. It's simple, really. I love you, you love me, we're back together and that's all there is to it."

"It's not and you know it. Does the word hallucination bring back any pleasant memories?"

"Don't worry-I am not giving you up and I will not go back on those medications."

"Ok, don't say I didn't warn you. The kids are going to insist you see the psychiatrist who is going to once again recommend medication. That means more pills and less thrills. Ok, that's enough about us for a while. Now what about Don? What did you find out about Don and his job?"

"Nothing yet. I'm working on it."

"Again with the old: working on it. I swear you must be working 2 fulltime jobs, if you are that busy working on it."

"No, the time wasn't right."

"There's no time like the present. Trust me, I know from experience. I'll talk to you later after you've spoken to Sissy. Just think over carefully what I said. And please don't say: Some of the best comments are the ones left unsaid." POP, and she was gone.

The traffic was still very heavy even at 2 pm. Frustrated with the traffic, Ben made an impulsive decision and called Bill, his high school classmate on the phone. Even though Ben had given them no prior notice, Bill was more than happy to hear from him, and Sally insisted they stop by for a visit. That's the kind of married couple they were. Ben took the address and programed it in Google Maps. They were only 15 minutes away though when they were only 5 minutes away, Google led them by a HUGE Frito-Lay Potato Chip Factory.

Then, they there were, in front of Bill and Sally's nice suburban home with the two Texans doing touch up work on their shrubs. Firecracker that she was, Sally was wearing her glitter gold Trump T-shirt. Bill was wearing a Texas Longhorn T-shirt. Yep, Texans through and through. Ben had kept track of Bill and Sally on Facebook, but had lost track of where they lived in Fort Worth. Bill and Sally had fled Minnesota's mind numbing winters soon after college and now officially considered themselves, true Texans. Their permafrost had melted off years ago.

In a way, the couple had always had been Texans, with their relentlessly optimistic view of moving forward. In the case of Bill and Sally (a realtor), this meant moving 20 times in 33 years of marriage. They believed that anyone could pull themselves up by their own, cowboy bootstraps, and so the two of them did, a little bit higher and better each year. Ben was in awe of their industriousness and positivity. As a cook, Sally was amazing. She quickly put together a meal for them all in about 23 minutes. Don must have timed it. After a pleasant conversation about all their kids, it was time to go. As Ben saw them in his rearview mirror, he tried to think of a word to describe the two of them. He thought it was the word gracious, even to 2 middle aged moochers like Don and himself, that hadn't even given them an hour's notice.

147 miles to go. Once he was in the car, Don was quickly asleep. No surprise. In spite of the great visit with Sally and Bill, Ben was still upset about his earlier conversation with Ann. To a large degree, she was right, but Ben was tired of pretending to everyone, he wasn't seeing Ann anymore. After

the big hullabaloo last time, Ben researched when people could be forced to take medications or see a shrink and Ben found under Minnesota State Law, the authorities could not make him take pills as long as he wasn't a danger to himself or others. Heck, he wasn't a danger, he was just feeling better!

Ben decided to pull off the road, one last time to pee and top off the tank. He could pee and Don could wake up. That guy could sleep like the best of them. It was too bad, napping was not an Olympic sport. Don would certainly qualify for at least a Bronze Medal thought Ben. He turned the car off at the pump and yawned loudly.

Don popped up: "Are we there yet?"

Ben decided Ann was right. He wanted to know why Don was in such a hurry to leave. He had a right to know. He decided to go for it:

"We're in Temple, less than 100 miles away from Austin. We passed some oil fields a while ago but I think I've seen more windmills than oil derricks in Texas. A better question is- why are we? As in, why are you running away from Minneapolis? I need the truth now. Did you get fired again?"

"Look, it's complicated. I'll tell you as soon I come back from the bathroom. Promise. I got to pee like a racehorse. Why don't you finish gassing up. I'll pay for gas all the way back home."

Don was fair in splitting costs. Always had been. Fair was fair.

"All right but no more lies or excuses." Finally, Ben was gonna get some answers.

Don came back a couple of minutes later with a couple of moon pies, a southern dessert treat made up of marshmallow stuffed between 2 chocolate dipped graham crackers. For some reason, people especially liked them with RC Cola, of which Don now had a 2 liter plastic bottle.

"Unbelievable."

"Hey, we can't get RC up north."

They walked back to the car and then were back on the road where they could talk privately: "Ok, we're alone, you can talk freely- time to fess up."

Don looked straight ahead: "I got fired and my wife doesn't know yet."

This was not a surprise to Ben but very bad news: "What did you do?"

"I violated some policies"

"When?" Ben figured it didn't matter which policies Don had violated. Only later, would he realize that not asking might have been a mistake.

"About 3 weeks ago…"

"3 weeks! Why haven't you told your wife?" Ben answered his own question: "Of course not, she thinks you're on a leave.."

Don shrugged his shoulders as if he didn't really have a choice. Such as it always was. This was never a good sign: "I just thought it would be more humane to ease her into it, this way."

"Are you insane?" Ben couldn't believe it. No, after being Don's friend for most of the last 45 years, he could believe it: "You gotta tell her right away. I can pull off the next exit and give you some privacy. You can't keep this a secret forever."

"I need to tell her in person. I was kind of hoping you would come with me when I did."

Then the knowledge hit Ben, Don wasn't just afraid, he was ashamed. "Look, I'm sorry I just can't do that. I'm your friend, I'm not your marriage counselor."

Don glanced at Ben and then looked at the Texas brown field plains: "I know that. I just thought it was worth a shot." Don stared ahead

As a relatively competent union attorney, Ben had one more question: "What are you going to do for health insurance?"

"That's a no brainer, I checked. As a qualifying event under COBRA, we can get it through her employer."

Ben thought Don's whole plan was a no brainer. Little did he know.

They were back in suburban heavy traffic only 53 miles to Austin and it was past 4 pm. Why was it so crowded driving into the city?

Ben thought it was time to give his sister a call:

"Hey Sis, it's your favorite brother." Ben was Fran's only brother, he had long ago worn out his tired old joke.

Fran ignored it: "Where are you? I've got Salmon to put on the grill and your favorite Velveeta Dip ready to melt." Velveeta cheese was an acquired taste and Ben had more than acquired it many years ago as a child. Grilled cheese, macaroni and cheese, cheese microwaved with picante sauce, their mom had made it all with Velveeta. It was still Ben's favorite cheese and it comforted him like nothing else. When melted, he called it his liquid gold. Fran had long recognized his continuing preference and one year for his birthday, gave him 4 lbs. (1800 grams) of what she considered plastic cheese. But her little baby brother now almost 60, still loved Velveeta, so like a good sister, she loaded up on the stuff when he came into town.

"We're in Georgetown now but my smart phone says traffic is heavy all the way to the Mopac Expressway. Better give us an hour."(It was only 30 miles but Austin had some of the worst traffic in the country)

"Ok, I won't start anything til you two finally get here.(Big sisters always note when siblings are late.) It will be good to see you. Say hello to Don for me."

"It will be good to see you and Theo, too. Bye"

Traffic in Austin was incredible and not in a good way. Superimpose a city that had tripled in size in 20 years, on a local highway system that was more clogged than the arteries of a prime surgical candidate, then it could only be Austin, Texas. Oh yes, then there were no east west through streets, either. Ben had marveled on previous visits that you see businesses across the Mopac Highway that you simply could not get to them in less than 20 minutes. Residents in the know, would go one way to do an errand and have to take a completely different route to get back. Remarkable, just remarkable.

Don had only been to Austin once before but, had still of course researched the BBQ scene on his other App: Best BBQ near and dear to me. There was Stubb's, Brown's, Cooper's, and Terry Black's. Don thought it was odd that that so many of the places had possessive names, but no matter. People were not only passionate but also possessive about their BBQ in Texas. But what really mattered to Don wasn't the name but the taste of the BBQ. He in his research had even found decent Breakfast BBQ at, Rudy's and allegedly decent BBQ Brisket even in a chain of Gas Stations, Buc-ee's, another Texas institution. Again with the possessive names.

Don was really awake now, almost giddy: "Can we go out for BBQ Breakfast?" They were staying overnight for a day or two with Fran and Theo.

"I'm sure we'll find time for BBQ at least once." (Ha, It wouldn't surprise Ben if they had BBQ, 4 times in the 2 days while they were in the Austin.) Don always said an elevated cholesterol was an elevated life.

Chapter 6

Go Fish

After getting off Mopac and taking a left underneath the expressway, they were there at his sister's, wearing all of their 1200 miles down to Austin.

"Benny! So good to see you." Sissy flew out of the house and grabbed him in what felt like a Heimlich maneuver from the front. Sissy had not seen her brother since his forced time in the psychiatric ward. She had come to visit. It was 4 months ago and Ben was so deeply depressed over the loss of Ann, the family wasn't sure he would make it without her.

But now 4 months later, he looked good and felt better.

"Benny, you look good, Don, you don't look so bad yourself. Come inside, y'all must be exhausted." Y'all? Really? Ben still thought of his favorite sister as a northerner but she and Theo had lived in Austin for over 30 years. But some of the neighbors still called them Yankees.

Home was a beautiful grey rambler with a mural on the outside where the carport used to be. The carport had been converted to a business office. Inside was a sleek contemporary Nordic style home with light wood floors and clean white walls. Her Minnesota roots still shined through. A piece of Lake Superior driftwood laid displayed as a natural sculpture in a wood entertainment center. A Table for 4 complete with wine glasses for all of them had been set on the table. (Light Danish Maple wood) Benny now understood why the neighbors felt the way they did about the upstart Minnesota Swedish Yankees.

Sissy wasted no time in setting the agenda: "Theo, Don has been cooped up in a car all day, Why don't you two go for a bike ride and be back in a hour before its dark? Ben and I will finish making the salad and grill the salmon." In an instant, Sissy had separated the warring and peaceful parties. Ben knew what discussion was coming next. He almost ducked involuntarily.

Theo and Don were both big bikers, they could easily ride more than 500 miles in a week, sometimes over a 100 miles in a day. Austin, except for the crazy drivers was a great place to bike. The city was extremely hilly.

Sometimes introduced as Kentucky's smartest man (Theo, never bragged about his intellect, even when the local NPR station limited how many times he could play quiz bowl each month) Theo had a generous soul and quickly offered Don first dibs on one of his 5 bikes. He even promised to take Don near several BBQs where if Don wasn't having BBQ tonight, he could still smell it so he could make an informed decision on where to eat some other time while in Austin. In a couple of minutes after the luggage was brought in, they were gone.

Chapter 7

Sisterly Talk

That left Sissy and Ben alone in the house and Ben defenseless.

"Let's get started with the salad." Fran was almost a chef when it came to making salads. She made her own salad dressing from scratch and used 5 kinds of vegetables. Fran had outlawed iceberg lettuce at her house (no nutritional value) and every salad had kale or spinach in it.

"Benny, you look good. You taking good care of yourself?" she asked professionally while she lightly massaged the spinach under the running water with her hands. She said this brought the vitamins out.

"Yeah, I'm feeling a lot better. I am eating more healthy and getting more sleep."

"Are you still taking your Haldol?" Again the professional voice. Haldol was a prescribed antipsychotic medication used to prevent hallucinations.

"My doctor hasn't said I still have to anymore." But what Ben left unsaid, is that he had stopped seeing the psychiatrist, weeks ago.

"Have you been having any hallucinations?" The combined all knowing, all telling older sister/social worker asked this question.

"You can use her name-its Ann remember? I've been meaning to talk to you about this- somehow – someway (Ben didn't pretend he knew how), Ann and I got back together." Gosh, this talk was even harder than Ben thought it was going to be.

"Oh, Benny... I can't believe it. Do you feel she's here now?" she stopped cutting the vegetables, put down the knife and stared intently at him.

"No, she's not. Look, we're both happier together. I am not going to lie to you about understanding how it happened, why it happened, it just did and I am glad it did. I am a lot happier."

"Have you told your doctor?"

Ben lifted his arms in frustration: "Look, Sissy, I don't need that doctor anymore. We're in a good place. Can't you just be happy for us?"

Fran sat down and she too brought up her hands: "I am happy that you are feeling better and that... somehow, you think you've reconnected with Ann. I just gotta tell you that this information is a lot to handle and it's really concerning."

"It concerns me and Ann, Nobody else."

"Have you told your kids?"

"I wanted to talk to you first. Unlike last time, will you let ME talk to MY kids first?" There was some bad history here between Fran and her brother. The first the kids heard about Ann's return was from their beloved Auntie Fran, not their Dad. It did not go well and it had taken a long time to get things back on track with the kids.

"I was really worried about you. I still am."

"Worry all you want. Just don't do it in front of my kids! We know what we're doing." Ben was a little harsher than he meant to be.

Ben paused, realized that his frustration had come out stronger than he intended. Ben knew he wasn't being entirely fair. Fran meant well, she always did. He apologized: "I'm sorry, Fran.

Just then Don and Theo walked in, conveniently so. They knew better than to walk into a Brother –Sissy argument that could be heard outside the door. Ben grabbed a glass of wine and walked into the backyard. Theo asked how the talk had gone. Fran grabbed the platter of uncooked salmon and thrust it to her husband: "Go Fish."

The rest of the meal was pretty quiet with occasional feeble attempts at civil conversation. Both Fran and Ben recognized this conversation wasn't over, not by a long shot.

Theo though, was an optimist, he tried to bring the conversation to neutral ground: "What are you two interested in seeing while you here? You know, it's been a while since we had any guests?"

Don was quick to answer. Maybe too quick and a little forced: "I'd sure like some BBQ while I'm here. You got any places nearby?"

Theo laughed, a genuine laugh: "Well, what a surprise. You just had BBQ. At Country Boy, we stopped on our bike ride, remember?"

Don's stomach wasn't embarrassed in the least: "That was just an appetizer to get my tummy acclimated to Texas BBQ."

Fran was insulted: "You knew we were having dinner here, why couldn't you wait?"

To Don, the answer was logical: "I was just building a base."

Ben had enough of trying to analyze Don's stomach, even after 40 years he still didn't understand where it came from or where it all went:

"You know, I would really like to see the Bat Cave while we are here in Austin. We've been talking about doing it forever."

The Bat Caves really did exist and were a popular local tourist attraction in Austin. There are hundreds of thousands (no exaggeration) of bats that congregate under the Congress Avenue Bridge and they make up the largest urban bat colony in the world. These are Mexican Free Tail bats and they typically emerge after sundown. Like sensible northerners who can afford to, they like to fly away for warmer climes when it gets colder. Thus, the bats winter in central Mexico.

Fran was in a peacemaking mood: "That sounds like fun. I can make a late dinner picnic. How do you want to spend the rest of the day?"

Some folks still believed in Austin's old slogan: "Keep Austin weird but more and more Austin reminded Ben as a larger version of Madison, Wisconsin but with much worse traffic. Ben tried making conversation again: "It might be fun to hit some of the quirky museums you've talked about. Later, we can all listen to live music at the Little Longhorn Museum when we're done watching the bats fly over our picnic."

Don had other ideas: "How about going out for breakfast tacos and then ride our bikes to Texas Hill Country"

Theo smiled then: "You're on. 100 miles- Loser pays!" Theo wanted to make sure there was more than enough time for Fran and Ben to workout whatever they needed to work out about Ann and be closer to being done with it. Not that they would ever be completely done with it. He was wise that way, too.

Fran thought the suggestion for the day made sense: "Sounds like a plan to me as long as you two bikers are back before 4 pm for the picnic." It was going to take a lot of time to get through to Ben, her baby brother.

Everyone agreed and the party petered out soon after. Fran and Don went to bed and Theo retreated to the computer world to play some Bridge.

Ben went into the backyard and looked at the early sunset. It was beautiful there and he admired the still blooming flowers. That wasn't something you would see in Minnesota by this time of year.

Fran had a nonfunctioning water fountain that she picked up at a garage sale that was quite large. They had to borrow their neighbors Ford pickup truck to get it back. Ben sat and felt the miles of his and Don's long trip weigh upon him. He recognized Fran's prized outdoor kaleidoscope but it was too late to be able to look through it. Ben made a mental note to carefully examine it the next day. He also saw dark outlines from Fran's rock collection. This was another thing that Fran and Ben shared in common was a fascination in, not geology but rather just interesting rocks that they picked up on the journey of their lives. The rocks symbolized something meaningful to both of them, but tonight Ben did not have a clue what it was.

Chapter 8

Ann Comes to Town

Now it was dusk, the barely visible shadows were still dancing to a very slow beat. Cars just returning from work, the traffic was that bad put on their headlights so they could avoid the rambling coyotes. Ben sat on the now slightly rusty glider that he had given them as a wedding anniversary gift many years ago. Back and forth. Squeak. Back and forth. Squeak. Ben felt his eyelids grow heavy and then he heard the POP.

"Told you, she would call me a type of hallucination."

"Hey Ann, so glad you are here now. Yeah, you were right." Ben didn't bother to open his eyes, he wouldn't have seen her anyways unless she was in virtual mode. To be honest, Ben preferred sometimes talking to Ann with his eyes closed. It reminded him of how things had been, it replayed the countless nights they spent in bed talking, long after turning the lights off. Sometimes, it felt like they were being verbally caressed by the other. Others might call it making love with their minds which to Ben sounded kinda cheesy. In any case, both Ben and Ann cherished those nights.

"Well, aren't I, usually?" Ben felt her warm smile.

Ben sighed: "Yes, Ann, you are always willing to admit when you are wrong- but of course you never are."

"Ha. How did you two end it?"

"Didn't you listen in? "

"Of course, not"

"We didn't end anything. We'll probably have a round 2, no survivors, wrestling cage match after the boys leave tomorrow for their big bike hike."

"You sound tired and a little angry."

"I am tired and a little angry. Not at you. I'm still angry at Sissy for starting this whole Pyscho-Bunko stuff with my kids and the doctors."

"Hey, don't you pick on my favorite sister in law. She's your older sister, that's her job! She believes she's looking out for you"

"Yeah, I know I do appreciate her, trying to look out for me. It's just she went a little too much social worky on me."

"Social Worky? Come on. Let it out. What's really going on?"

"Just my usual worries, that people won't understand this-Us. I still wish, we had just kept it a secret from everyone, when we got back together. It didn't end up so well last time when we told them at first. Why would things be any different this time?"

"Gotta admit, I'm not really sure. (Ben loved Ann's honesty. Always had) It just feels different. Maybe now they'll all be more accepting because they saw how bad things got for you when they tried to put the Psychiatric Kibosh on us."

"Maybe…Ah Ann, sorry but I'm so tired, I'm afraid my eyelids are going to fall off. Can we go to bed together and pick this up tomorrow?"

"Sure, honey."

So Ben picked up his body and they softly went to bed.

CHAPTER 9

THE GREAT AWAKENING

The next morning, the four of them went out for breakfast after 3 of them turned down Ben's generous offer to make Velveeta omelets. Jose's was located underneath Mopac Expressway, and had an early morning special of migas with coffee for $4.99. It consisted of corn tortillas scrambled with eggs, tomatoes, chilies, onions and topped with cheese. Real cheese. Jose's was tired but clean and appeared to be a converted IHOP or some similar closed restaurant. There was a strong smell of coffee brewing and 2/3 of the patrons were Hispanic. Jose's opened at 6 am and for people who didn't have time to wait, Pepe's offered a breakfast special one migas and large coffee to go for only 2 bucks. It attracted a hungry and hardworking crowd.

These were the workers who cut your lawn, cleaned your house, did construction, took care of your kids/seniors, repaired your roof and basically did all the low paying, difficult hard labor that the Anglos no longer wanted to do. It wasn't necessarily fair (Usually wasn't) but it's what we did as a society to keep things working without a second glance.

Intent on eating his meal, while it wasn't BBQ, Don was more than satisfied and kept a copy of the bill so he could be reimbursed by Theo after

| 69

the great Texas Hill Country bike race they were about to have. They drove home and they all assumed their battle stations, Theo / Don biking, and Fran/ Ben discovering the quirky museums that kept Austin weird. Theo and Don were off quickly on their bikes. Then, it was just the two left home, no really, 3 of them if you included Ann.

Then Ann POPPED up in his bedroom where Ben had gone to get his sunglasses:

"Good morning, sunshine, got a fun day planned?"

"Morning. Sort of. We're going to see some of the quirkier museums in Austin. We've already seen the State Capitol, LBJ Presidential and Bullock Texas State History Museums, all together, a bunch of times, remember?" The nice thing about having a long term partner, is the shared history that the parties can jointly remember. The total memory is truly bigger than the 2 separate parts. Usually but not always. Sometimes it does the opposite and the couple makes the same mistake over, and over and over again. As in: "Of course we can fix this repair issue ourselves." And "Sure we can leave our car here overnight." But joint snafus are part of the shared history, too. Ten years out, remembering these errors might be amusing. Sometimes. All right, almost never.

This morning, Ann was not in the mood to be reminded again of some unmedicated Texans' eccentricities:

"Yeah, BORING! Let me summarize for you, Texas is a big state, Texas is a historic state, Texas is a unique state."

"Yep, that pretty much sums it up. Fran promised some different ones this time, including the Cathedral of Junk and the Museum of the Weird. I added the O. Henry Museum/Home of one of my favorite authors."

Ben did love to read even if he kept it well hidden to the outside world. Thankfully Ann was a big reader, too. It was something else that the 2 of them loved to share. When Ann was alive, they spent many quiet nights just reading together in the same room. Not much talking. Then again talk was unnecessary. Both believed in a philosophy that a life well read, is a life well spent. They were happy that their kids and soon their grandchildren would have a love of books, too. (If Ann and Ben had anything to do with it.)

"Ben, I've been thinking. If you fessed up to Fran, you need to call the kids, at the very least Esther before they hear from Fran."

Ben considered her advice and realized as in most things, she was right: "That's a good suggestion, I'll try her later today." Of the two kids, Esther, an Orthodox Jew, would probably be the most open minded, surprising as that sounded. Their son Larry was a high powered litigator in LA. Sue was, well, Sue. When Ben told the kids, the first time, that he was seeing, rather than just thinking about Ann again, Larry freaked. Esther, on the other hand, accepted as part of her deep faith, that there were things in this life that we could never understand, but that we could still accept. Then there was also the "other one" their daughter Sue, whom they had been estranged (Such a fancy French word that didn't explain the anguish a parent felt.) from for such a very long time. It was hard to talk about their relationship with Sue so most of the time they didn't. That was the nice thing about

|71

your children becoming adults, you no longer had to. Except when you HAD to.

"You know, Ann, it would help me with the kids and Fran if you could speak to them, too, so I'm not hanging out there all by myself."

"Still worried about what other people think? I wish I could, but that might over load the circuits if I did that. Might start a trend. Imagine how many Spirits would be talking to how many people if there was no limit?" Ben couldn't. "That's why we, Spirits are limited to one customer at a time and that's why only you can hear me." Made sense. Sort of. On the other hand it might be Ann's way of avoiding some certain unpleasantness.

"Well, could we at least schedule regular visits for us at set times?" Ben had been jumpy at first when he started hearing from Ann. He never knew when she would be popping in. Now, just like before when she was alive, he valued her advice and missed her if he went too long without hearing from her.

Ann sighed: "Wouldn't that be nice but with the traffic in the cloud, 5G network upgrade, and the weather (Strong storms affected performance), I don't think I can do that, sorry. I will continue try and show up as often as I can every day."

"Thanks, Honey."

"I'll let you get to it." POP.

There was going to be no rest for the already weary.

Chapter 10

Time to Go

So, Fran was ready to go, as usual. Social workers were not almost always the first ones there but always the most prepared. Fran was an exception. She was almost always on time. Ben was looking forward to this tour of the truly odd. Ben enjoyed sightseeing with his sister. She had a positive attitude and had a wide ranging curiosity of the world. Since neither of them had partners who enjoyed traveling as much, the siblings had even traveled to distant locales together. The only problem were the HUGE suitcases that Sissy insisted on bringing on every trip. Fran usually insisted on a minimum of 2 suitcases and each were the size of a refrigerator. Frannie insisted that the suitcases being on wheels made them easy for Ben to maneuver. But as Ben pointed out, the spinner wheels did no good on cobble or dirt roads full of potholes and Ben believed he had gotten carpal tunnel, lifting them, on their last foreign trip together. Seriously.

They decided to start with the Cathedral of Junk, after calling Vincent, the owner, to ensure it was open and that there was space available for them. After all, it isn't every day that a guy takes 60 tons of junk and builds something uniquely beautiful in his suburban backyard. The artist Vincent started building it in 1989 and one can only imagine what happened initially with the neighbors. While the neighbors were justifiably upset, in Texas there is a constitutional right to be able to piss your neighbors off. So it's still standing. It is structurally sound and has several period rooms, a green room, a pink, and a red one among others. It's about 30 feet tall, has stairways and a slide made from surplus tile for the kids. There's even a cathedral spire shaped partial roof.

No pun intended, but Ben found it awe inspiring, especially after talking to the artist Vincent, who created it. Others found it just plain awful.

In keeping with the Keep Austin Weird theme of the day, their next stop was to the Museum of the Weird. It reminded Sissy of the old dime museums or side show attractions at the State Fair. It had a plethora of items from UFO and Big Foot to shrunken heads exhibits and even a nifty gift shop. The frozen Minnesota Ice Man was a particular hit for both of them. It brought back some not so fond memories of Minnesota winter storms and still being made by their mother to trudge to grade school. By the time, they were done with the museum, both were ready for some bland suburban food served in a comfortable, well cushioned setting so they stopped at Olive Garden of all places.

With a glass of wine in hand, Fran was ready to talk about Ann again: "Look, I'm sorry if I came down so heavy; but I was worried about you. If you're happy and doing well, that's all that matters." Fran couldn't bring herself to mention Ann's name today. Whatever.

Ben was too tired for a drink and besides, they were supposed to hit a honky tonk bar later. He wanted it to be a short round two. Ben knew that it wouldn't end here. He opened up first with: "Ok, can we at least agree to respectfully disagree? Let's just move forward. Listen, the three of us just want to get going to Sedona as quickly as we can. So we probably are going to leave tomorrow or the following day."

"You just got here. It isn't because of what I said about your wife, is it?"

"Of course not." Ben lied. Never let truth get in the way of a good family relationship: "Don is in a hurry to get to El Paso. He wants to spend a day in El Paso's sister city Ciudad Juarez, Mexico getting some custom cowboy boots and some prescription pharmaceuticals that are much cheaper there." This was even bigger lie, Ben hadn't even talked to Don about any of this. But Ben knew his friend would back his story up. Always had.

"He's getting only legal stuff, right? Nothing herb related right? Besides, if all he wants are some classy cowboy boots, he can go to the Lucchese boot outlet store. El Paso Texas is the boot making capital of the United States, you know." Ben didn't know that but he did already know after his sister lived in Texas for over 30 years: Texas had the most oil, cattle, horses, cowboys, cow boy boots, Texas BBQ was the best, and just simply put- Texas was the best State ever. Having relatives in the great state of Texas could be quite annoying.

By this time Ben was ready for something, anything, that was not totally Texas related. "How about a visit to the O. Henry museum now?"

"Sounds fine to me." Sissy made the concession grudgingly. So off they went to the O. Henry House and Museum.

William Porter better known under his pen name O. Henry was Ben's favorite short story writer. He was author of such stories as The Gift of the Magi and The Ransom of Red Chief. He died young at age 47 in 1910 but in

| 75

that short time, he wrote close to 400 short stories. He lived in Austin for a short period of time where he worked as a bank teller until he was fired for alleged embezzlement. (He later served time in federal jail for the alleged crime. Then again, what good famous author is not a thief at the very least of words?) But he could sure write, and his stories were full of compassion and humor. He was also an excellent illustrator and cartoonist.

The O. Henry Museum was housed in the small former residence of William Porter. It being Texas, visitors were requested to wear soft shoes (ie no cowboy boots) to avoid damaging the soft wood floors. Both Fran and Ben were moved by the simple exhibits of a talented man who led a wild life and then died too young from cirrhosis of the liver. So many books left to write. It was a vivid reminder that too much talent cannot survive too much need, in this case alcohol.

Chapter 11

What You Don't See, is What You Get.

Then feeling tired (From the wine?), they went home to recharge, really to take a nap. Meanwhile the boys were racing along and had made it to Johnson City. It was less than 50 miles each way in some of the prettiest Texas Hill Country. There, they ate at a diner at the lunch counter and following a beef commercial, they toured the boyhood home of LBJ. President Johnson had been dirt poor as a youth and didn't even have electricity in his house. Congressman Johnson vowed to change this for others and by golly, he did. While he made a bad situation, much worse, in Vietnam, he did truly care about the poor and that's what his "Great Society" programs attempted to help. Otherwise as Johnson noted, what's a presidency for?

The trouble for the boys occurred when they started racing back at around 2 pm when Theo hit a dead deer with his very expensive carbon fiber bike. He hadn't seen it because he was posed with his hands on the racing handles and he couldn't see what was directly in front of him. Being carbon, the bike didn't bend, it shattered and Theo's ankle looked very bad. It had quickly grown to the size of a large softball. Theo hadn't seen the deer because, he had his fore arms positioned together in such a way that it blocked his vision straight ahead. While he didn't see the deer, he sure felt it. Thankfully a Good Samaritan in a truck stopped and loaded up Theo and took what was left of his bike to the hospital which was ironically also called Good Samaritan. Don had called Fran to reassure her that although Theo's bike was shattered, his body probably wasn't. Fran jumped into her car and rushed to the hospital, forgetting to tell Ben what had happened.

Ben woke up an hour later and found the home eerily quiet. No one answered his call. It reminded him of how their townhome sounded or didn't sound after Ann died. The silence grew so loud back then that he took to leaving on CNN all the time. Then again now it was an election year so he left the television off.. After opening a Doctor Pepper, Ben decided this quiet time would be a good opportunity to call their daughter Esther: "Hey kid, how are you?" Even after living for 26 years, Esther was still the kid to her father. In some ways she always would be. Parents just couldn't help it.

"Hi Dad, I think a better question is where are you? You make it to Frannie's yet?"

"Yep, made it here all safe and sound yesterday, got time to talk?" Esther was a social worker just like her aunt. Social workers always had too much work to do.

"For my favorite dad, I've always got time. How are you feeling?"

"Great. I put 20 lbs. back on, I'm exercising every day and I'm sleeping much, much better."

That's good, how's the weather?"

"Funny, you should mention that. It still feels like summer here which is lovely but I miss Fall most of all.. That crunching of the leaves, the whispering in the wind, do you know what I mean?"

Esther's dad was leading up to something, Esther could feel it. Like her mom, she was intuitive.

"Remember how I was hearing your mom, after she passed?" Oh brother, this did not sound good at all to Esther.

"Well, I started hearing your mom again and several months ago we started seeing, I mean hearing each other mostly, again." Ben cleared his throat in the hopes that would make the above sound more reasonable.

Ever the clinical social worker, Esther still had one more question for her dad: "What does your Psychiatrist say?"

"He's not worried, he hasn't said a word." That was because Ben had fired him several months before.

"Are you still taking your meds?"

"I'm taking what I'm supposed to." Depending on your point of view this, was either again a complete lie or serious omission because he hadn't been taking his meds in months.

"Have you told Larry or Fran yet?" Esther knew that her brother Larry would blow a gasket. Ben wanted to firm up his family defenses before calling the busiest litigator in LA.

"I let Fran know but you know how hard it is to get ahold of Larry." This could have been true if Ben had tried contacting his son who was eternally busy.

"What does Fran say?"

"Well, she's not legally opposed to it." This meant she wasn't considering legal action. Yet…

"Uh-Huh." Esther sounded doubtful.

"Look honey, I know it sounds strange and I don't know how it happened but we're back together, somehow. I haven't felt this good since before your mother died. You of all people, should understand that just because we can't understand everything, that doesn't mean we shouldn't accept it. "

Esther thought he was trying to relate it to her strong religious views in a poorly stated, double negative sort of way.

"Look dad, I'm not going to pretend I am happy about it, but if you're happy and healthy that's all that matters to me."

"While I'm not asking for permission, I do appreciate your support." Ben was still more than a little defensive.

"Ok, just make sure you suck it up now and call Larry. You might as well call Sue, too. Get it over and done with. You don't want either him and Fran trying to go legal on you again."

This was enough for Ben and Ann. They now had at least one daughter who was in their corner or at the very least edging towards it.

CHAPTER 12

THEY GO BAT SH*T CRAZY

Fran and what been self-styled bike warriors until the accident, ultimately showed up at their home about 3:30pm. Theo had his foot in a boot and was on strong pain killers. His beautiful sky blue carbon bike laid shattered in several boxes in the garage. His ankle was broken and he now had 4 pins and a plate that could set off alarms at the airport security gates. Theo was flying the friendly skies high on the medication, so Fran decided the two of them would stay at home that night.

Ben and especially Don, were still up for the bats and googled the location of the Congress Street Bridge. Ben put Don to work researching the best place to get BBQ near there, as they were leaving for El Paso tomorrow. As predicted, Don had been more than ok with leaving tomorrow but insisted on one more beef extravaganza. Ben was grateful he had only soup and salad at lunch. They decided to leave for dinner in about half an hour.

Ben had time to call Larry but he wanted to get Ann's perspective before starting the shouting match with their youngest child. Ben and Larry always had a challenging relationship. Larry's high school guidance counselor described Larry as "highly spirited." That was a nice way of putting it. Ben at times was inclined to believe his son took P.I.T.A. (pain in the ass) pills at least once every day, sometimes twice. On the other hand, he cared about his parents and family very deeply. Like a lot of men, he just kept his feelings well hidden. Why he did, Ben did not know.

Don and Ben met outside and drove to Beefy's located downtown, near the bridge where the bats hung out. For fun, they decided to take local streets and avoid the highway. Austin has few east west streets and to make matters worse, both east west and north south streets have numbered streets which are quite confusing even to native Texans. Eventually with Google's help they found their way. They found some decent parking and recognized Beefy's by the line outside. It wasn't even 5 pm. They went through the quasi cafeteria line and savored their beef brisket and baked beans in the back patio.

Yes, it was yet another BBQ again, with the picnic tables outside, and paper towels instead of napkins. For some unknown reason, many male operators felt using paper towels instead of napkins was more authentic. In reality, all it did was cost more and work less. The paper towels generally just moved the BBQ sauce around and did not clean it. This type of dining option would have a hard time making it in the cold of the North. Don's belch, more like a fog horn, announced that he finally had enough food to eat. They decided to walk to the park by the bridge that according to Trip Advisor was the best place to view the spectacle unless you were on the river. Unfortunately, several hundred other people had googled the same thing and were already sitting or picnicking by the river's edge. Still they managed to find a spot and sit down.

It was almost dusk, then all at once, there were over 600,000 bats (no exaggeration) pouring out from underneath the bridge like an alien invasion force. It looked like a never ending wave of bats. It took between 30 to 45 minutes for them all to leave. It was one of the most remarkable things Ben and Don had ever seen, but neither could describe it in proper detail. You couldn't hear anything other than the bat wings flapping and the bats made sounds that were up to 2 times above what humans could hear. Pretty amazing. In terms of how Ben and Don would rate it as something to see. They argued for a while, but eventually agreed it was more interesting than Mt. Rushmore, but not as moving as the Grand Canyon. In any case, it was a remarkable sight.

They hit a honky tonk to talk about what they had seen. Thankfully, the joint had cheap cold beer (Don's favorite Shiner Bock) and loud music. Even better, they couldn't hear each other talk. This made their conversation easier even if it was less productive. After all it was a well-known fact that guys especially when their shouting was lubricated with beer, simply did not listen well. So by 9 pm, they were ready to go back to Sissy's house.

Ben promised to have coffee early with his sister before leaving, and Ben and Don agreed on another 7 am start. It had been a busy, too busy, 36 hours in Austin.

Ben took off his glasses and decided to take a short nap before getting ready to go to sleep. He hadn't intended on doing it this way but there wasn't always someone to nudge him into going to bed. Tonight though, he did. Ann finally POPPED in. He wasn't sure how long he had been asleep before she came:

"Come on sleepy head, you can't sleep until you brush your teeth and change into your pajamas. I know it was a full day but that's no excuse for poor sleep hygiene."

"Hey Ann, I tried to stay awake for you but just couldn't do it any longer. I'm not the party animal I used to be, who could party or study all night, and then take an exam the next day. I love you but I'm sooo sleepy."

"Yes, you have a big day tomorrow if you're going to drive all the way to El Paso. That's almost 600 miles from here, all in the Great State of Texas. But listen here, I had some things to ask you about."

"Can't this wait until tomorrow? I can't help that I am so tireeed."

"Buck up and wake up!" That was what Ann said to the kids when they didn't want to get up in the morning for school.

"Yes ma'am." Ben felt the wake up gears finally moving. He sat up and put on his glasses. Ben saw he was still in his clothes: "What did you want to talk about?"

"Everything. First, how was your day?"

"Fine." Ben's sleepy mind thought one word answers might give her the hint that indeed Ben was really sleepy. No such luck.

"Second, did you call our daughter Esther?"

"Yes."

"How did she take it?"

"Fine."

| 85

"Did you call Sue?"

"Nope."

"Can you answer anything in more than a monosyllabic answer?"

"Maybe."

"Did you call Larry?"

"I'm working on it."

"Good progress- up to 4 words now."

"I can do it tomorrow, it's late."

"Nice try cowboy, its 2 hours earlier in LA so it's only 8 pm for him. He's probably just getting home from work."

"Too tired, I won't be able to carry on a conversation."

"Given your verbal history, it's probably would be for the best. SO CALL HIM NOW ANYWAYS." The discussion had turned into a red alert directive.

So Ben did what all wise husbands do when their loving spouses order them to telephone their sons, he made the call after taking a big wake up breath:

"Larry, how you doing?.... That big of a case… How long has the Jury had it?… Listen, I've been thinking about you and just wanted to give you a call before I went to sleep....I care about you, too, (Since his Kidney cancer, Larry was much more affectionate.) I'm fine.....Listen your Mom and I have reconnected again and we thought you should know...Yes, I'm still taking the meds I'm supposed to (Ben felt less guilty lying to Larry than his sister. After all, Larry was an attorney, he should be used to people lying to him)... NO, I'm not going to talk to the Psychiatrist about this...Well, I am not being STUPID......I'm just doing what's best for me and trying to let you know..... Whatever. STILL LOVE YOU, TOO!" Ben hung up the phone with authority.

"Now that wasn't so hard, was it?"

"Yeah, it went better than I thought." Ben was being sarcastic.

"Did he make any legal threats this time?"

"No, but he did say he wasn't going to bail me out this time when something bad happened. That son of ours sometimes has a strange way of showing he loves us."

"Well, that's still progress. Doesn't sound like legal proceedings are really imminent. Seriously, I'm glad you got this out of the way and that Larry heard it from you."

"Can I try to go to sleep, now?"

"Of course, just change out of your clothes and brush your teeth, first, love you."

"I love you and sleep, too."

Chapter 13

On the Road Again

At 6 am, Fran was already up making breakfast for everyone. While it was quite thoughtful, Ben believed it was the fear of Velveeta, roaming wild and free, that convinced her to get up early.

"Hey Sis, anybody else up?"

"I heard Don puttering, but Theo is still in LA LA land."

"How's he feeling?"

"Sore, not just his body but sore also, that Don won the race."

"Fran, I just wanted to thank you for how considerate you and Theo have been to us. Both Don and I really appreciate it. I'm lucky to have you as a sister."

"I'm lucky, too. When are you coming back?"

"It's your turn to come up to Minnesota. How about a visit to the Minnesota State Fair followed by a joy ride up to the family cemetery in Grand Forks and then Winnipeg, Canada for their Folk Festival? It's not much further."

"Sounds ambitious, I like it. You call me when you get to El Paso?"

"Promise. You say goodbye to Theo for us." He hugged his sister. Ben hadn't generally done that before Ann died, but well, he felt different about things now.

"Don, time to go." He yelled in his best guy voice. "Your boots and pills are waiting."

"Ready to initiate launch procedures." Don carried his duffle bag out.

"Wanted to thank you and Theo for your hospitality…Tell him we can have a rematch in Minnesota. Loser pays for lunch at Cecil's Deli in St. Paul."

"Sounds like a plan. Can I make you a coffee and breakfast burrito to go?" And with that, Fran gave Don a hug, too. After all these years, he was part of the family. Don didn't have the heart to refuse the breakfast. He could always dump it when they hit a gas station. So began their 600- mile voyage across the great state of Texas.

Chapter 14

Texas is a BIG State.

After getting settled in and safely away from Ben's sister, Don asked if he should google the route.

"Nope. Don't need to. It's really simple. We take Highway 10 West all the way to Phoenix and El Paso is our first overnight. Its 576 miles all in Texas."

"Wow, that's a long ride."

"Yes, remember how we used to see travel advertisements for Texas, a whole another country? Well for a while it was. From 1836 after declaring Independence from Mexico to 1845 when they joined the United States, Texas was an independent country called the Republic of Texas."

"Did not know that but then again, didn't need to."

"Fair enough"

They drove in silence for a long while on Hwy 10 W. There were a lot of oil derricks once they got out of Hill Country. It was flat brown country with a lot of cattle too. If it hadn't been for oil, it would have been a poor country. Now with times changing, there were almost as many 300 feet tall silent wind turbines as oil derricks. That was the thing about good long term friends, you didn't just share memories, you could share that silence, too.

After 2 hours, Don had a question: "How far is it from Austin to Phoenix?"

"1000 miles."

"How far from Phoenix to Sedona?"

"About 120 miles, but it's a beautiful drive. Uphill and curvy. Bored yet?"

"Yep."

"Wanna stop?"

"Nope."

So they kept driving. For another hour. Eventually their gas tank was close to empty and Ben's bladder was again almost overflowing. Ben's urologist was right- coffee does not make a bladder any happier or larger. He and his bladder decided unilaterally to stop at the next exit and take a break.

They were in Ozona, Texas now still on Highway I-10W. Besides the Crockett County Courthouse, there was the Crockett County Museum and most importantly, the Wagon Wheel BBQ. Ozona was named after the clear air there (ie Ozone) and it was literally the only town in Crockett County. They had been on the road for over 3 hours and Don's stomach was more than ready for an early lunch. Ben gave in but was hopeful he could get something different than BBQ. Housed in a converted gas station, they went with the BBQ but even Ben appreciated the fine serving of beef brisket and sausage. Both were pretty good beef- Second best BBQ they had so far (well spiced.) and Ben was again tempted to push some cholesterol controlling Lipitor on Don. Only 320 miles until El Paso.

That Don had fallen asleep after every meal, was no surprise to Ben by now. Ben let his mind wander while he semi-paid attention to the road. After a while, he began to think about the forks in the road. Not on the highway, he was traveling now but the major decisions, he had made, sometimes without much thought. But that's life. He wondered what his life would have been like if he gone to the Iowa Creative Writers Workshop instead of going to law school.

This was long before he had met Ann and fallen in love. He remembered feeling at the time he applied to the writing program, that he couldn't emotionally or financially, just go to study, the craft of writing. He just wasn't that good and he felt that he had no safety net if it didn't work out. Heck, he was his own safety net for there was no money in his family. If he went to law school in Minnesota, he could still live at home if he couldn't swing an apartment and he could still work at the grocery store which paid fairly well. Maybe he could get a job with a law firm or nonprofit and work in the summers. But writing? How could he support himself and family? (He had looked at the probability of getting married and the odds ultimately were good.) He had no connections or money to support him. When it came right down to it. Again, he just wasn't that good of a writer and wasn't willing to risk it. For that matter, he wasn't that good of a typist either. Besides, Iowa nightlife/winters didn't intrigue him. At all.

Instead, he took the usual route for perspiring Jewish undergraduates who weren't interested in medical school, he bit the bullet and reconsidered law school after getting his history degree. There he could still write, speak, research, fight injustice Monday through Friday, weekends free and have a variety of different employment options. It would still be acceptable to his family who valued education, who like himself, knew nothing about the already vast oversupply of attorneys. To make matters worse many, many other perspiring undergraduates had the same idea. So many so that the United States ended up with more than 3 times more attorneys then were needed. Many graduated law school seriously in debt. Two hundred thousand dollars in debt was not that unusual. For those, it was a heavy burden in more ways than one.

Still, he felt pretty fortunate. He and Ann had built a good life in Minneapolis. He wondered how things would have worked out if he and Ann had followed Fran's advice and moved to Austin when the kids were little. But Ann had a decent job at United Healthcare and Ben doubted there was much need for a union attorney in Texas. He just couldn't behave or dress well enough to play at being a management attorney. Now only 200 miles to go until they reached El Paso.

Bored by the bland brown land scape, Ben looked up. There were flattened, horizontal pillow clouds in the skies except for one that seemed to have a beehive coming out of it. It reminded Ben of when Ann put her hair up for a costume party. He chuckled at the memory, from many years ago.

This memory in turn reminded him of his last session with the psychiatrist. The good doctor advised him that the hallucination, i.e. Ann could, ultimately, be dangerous to his mental psyche which otherwise was pretty stable.

"Why is that? It's not as if she's advising me to rob a bank or hurt someone."

"Because over time, your mind won't be able to distinguish between what's in your imaginary world and what's in the real physical world."

For a minute, Ben wondered the real difference was but thought himself wise not to share this thought with the psychiatrist.

The good doctor just wanted to increase Ben's dose of Haldol. Ben hated the side effects of the sedation and its resulting side effects that included constipation. He wasn't really surprised though. When you got right down to it, all drugs were side effects- the question was, did the good side effects outweigh the bad ones? But what Ben hated most of all was the doctor's attempt to build a chemical wall between he and Ann. That just wasn't right.

"Doc, let me ask you this, do you think we as humans perceive everything that is going around us?"

"No, we can't.."

Ben interrupted him: "Exactly, just like computers, we accept and use things we don't understand." (Ben realized the computer analogy was a bad one, but it was all he had on such short notice and Ben was trying to make an important point.)

"That's true." Psychiatrists did try to affirm their patients when they could. It was better for the patients and better for repeat business that in turn enlarged the doctors' pocketbooks.

"Doctor, I apologize for getting so personal, but do you believe in God?"

"Yes, of course.."

"Have you ever personally seen or heard God? "

The good doctor began to fidget: "Why no, but that doesn't mean a Supreme Being does not exist."

"Exactly." Ben thought he had just made an important point but like a lot of things, he wasn't sure what it was. Still to his credit, Ben pushed whatever his point was forward: "Ann brings me comfort whether she's real or not. We had a good thing going together when Ann was alive and we have a good thing going now. Sorry Doc, given a choice between sticking with you or her, I'm sticking with Ann."

So that's when Ben fired the doctor and told him graciously that his services were no longer required. To Ben's thinking, he had a choice of a world with or without Ann. He choose Ann. Ben didn't regret his choice at all. (Not one bit.)

The clouds continued to roll around as did the tumbleweeds racing along their car. Ann and the travel books were right: Texas is a big country.

Don finally woke up: "Are we there yet?"

"Almost" Ben replied. He was getting bored so he thought he would start an argument to pass the time:

"I need to advise you that we are going into a BBQ Free zone. Dinner, if we get there in time, is going to be Mexican."

But it didn't work. Don and his stomach had strong objections. Don and Ben had many arguments over the years. Ben liked to say they had known each other for 40 years and been friends for almost 30 of them.

In high school, once, Don and Stan almost got Ben suspended from school by calling the Assistant Principal and informing him that Ben's brother had been in a serious car accident. According to the call, Ben was needed at the hospital. Ben informed the Principal that he didn't even have a brother but the Principal insisted he leave school for the emergency, only confirming later that Ben, indeed, did not have a brother. While the school officer was convinced Ben or his friends were behind this stunt, they couldn't pin it on him. Those were the days.

So 40 years later they were cruising at 79 mph, where the speed limit was 75, on Highway 10 West flying to El Paso. Less than 100 miles to go.

"You really wanna buy cowboy boots in Juarez?"

"Yep."

"They're uncomfortable, expensive and hard to walk in."

"Yep but at least I can get them in alligator skin there. They'll look really cool. Maybe I'll be able to see my reflection in the boots."

"I don't even know if you can drive in those things." Although that wasn't much of an issue there. Don did not like to drive and besides, they were in one of Ben's prized possessions, his 2007 SRX Cadillac. Just then suddenly, the radiator was possessed and cracked. The car, slowly but authoritatively, rolled to a stop on the side of the interstate.

What to do? Ben had dumped his AAA coverage in favor of a cheaper SPELCO $7.99 per month towing coverage special to save money. But what was special was it covered tows only up to 10 miles. They were miles from anything. Ben gave the auto club a call from his cellphone.

"Hello Mr. Ben Diberg, how can we assist you today?

"That's Ryberg. Spelled R Y B E R G."

"Mr. Ben Dyberg Spelled DYBERG, can I please have your membership number and date of birth?"

"It's Ryberg like Rye toast without the E. My membership number is 13246759A346, my date of birth is 12-23-59."

"What kind of car?"

"a 2007 SRX Cadillac."

"Serial Number?"

"I'll have to look." Ben walked around his car on the sort of busy freeway and found the number on the front part of the left dashboard looking through the windshield. "It's 387640KB74902234. When, if ever, are you going to help me?"

"Patience is more than a virtue, Mr. Diberg. Is Mrs. Diberg available, perhaps she can take over this call?

"She died 6 months ago"

"Oh, I'm so sorry Mr. Diberg. Our records do not reflect that. On behalf of the Spelco Family of Companies, let me extend our condolences to you." There is a couple second delay then: "There you are but your name is Ryberg... Do you wish me to correct it for our records now?"

"Good Lord, Woman, all I want is a tow truck!"

"No reason to shout. I see you have our Basic membership. Would you like to upgrade it for a small fee at the end of our call?

"I JUST WANT MY FREAKING TOW TRUCK!"

Mr. Diberg, I will remind you that Spelco has a strict no harassment policy.. if you continue in this vein with such abusive language, I will have no choice but to end this call and immediately terminate your membership without a refund."

That would leave them nowhere, no tow truck, somewhere about 75 miles from El Paso: "Please don't. I'm sorry- it's just so frustrating being in the middle of nowhere…"

"No worries, Spelco would never leave their members in the lurch. Just give me your approximate location and we'll have a tow truck out for your complimentary 10 mile tow."

"But we're 75 miles from civilization… 10 miles will get us nowhere. Well actually we're right at exit 29 near nothing!"

"Sorry, 10 miles is all you are authorized for under the terms of your membership. Tell you what, I'll send the tow truck and you can work it out with him."

"Ok, thanks how long should it be?"

"I just checked and he said less than 1 hour."

"Thanks."

"Thanks for being a member of the Spelco family. Press 2 if you want to take a short 10 minute customer satisfaction survey."

Ben wasn't interested.

Chapter 15

The Repair is in the Details

Salvation came about 1 hour and fifteen minutes later. Terry's Auto World drove up in a old Chevy club tow truck.. And right now, Terry was the important person in the Caddy's world. Terry took a quick look and confirmed the radiator was toast:

"I can replace it if you want. I gotta a junkyard in the back of the station with a rear ended 2009 SRX Caddy in it. I can pull the radiator off that." He wiped his hands.

"How much would that cost?" Ben thought a straight forward approach would work best.

"Well, I can tow your car, remove and dispose of the old radiator and put in a new used radiator, all for $900. I could finish it by tomorrow."

"How much would a new one cost?" Don's question was not helpful.

"Well, I suppose you could pay me $250 to tow you to the Chevy/GMC dealer in El Paso and then have them order you a new one that would take several days to get there from the warehouse in Fort Worth, costing about $3000 just for parts not including installation…"

This was getting nowhere, fast. Ben interrupted and spoke quickly: "You know $900 is a bargain and I'd be happy to pay. Is there a town nearby, you can drop us off and we can spend the night?"

"Looks like you'll be spending the night in Van Horn, Texas, one of the furthest west cities in the Central Time Zone. They have The Hotel El Mountain" which is one of the finest hotels and restaurants in these parts. They serve a mean pistachio crusted baked chicken. Decent drinks, too."

"Sounds like a good plan. Don, what do you think?"

"Like we don't have much of a choice"

"That's the spirit. Terry, we'll take you up on your generous offer."

So while Terry hooked up the car to be towed, Don and Ben got their suitcases out of their chariot and climbed into the front seat. It was cramped but at least 5 minutes later, they were on their way.

Terry was in a good mood: "Did I mention that my wife's family owns the hotel and Juanita is the chef?"

"Gosh, Terry that must have slipped your mind. No problem. How long have they owned it?"

"About 20 years, they bought it in the 90's"

"Juanita's dad had retired from the military, come home here and was looking for something to do. He treats the hotel as his miniature air base. Everything has to be in order. Great food though. Ok, if we drop Caddy off first? I usually have dinner there on Wednesday when Juanita makes my favorite chicken."

"Hey, no problem for us, besides you're driving."

Terry dropped off the Caddy quickly, and then they were off to the El Mountain which was only 2 minutes away. It was a beautiful hotel built sometime in the 40's or 50's and it had an attractive lobby, the kind one could still see sometimes in old black and white movies. They gave Don and Ben the Friends and Family Rate and their 2 rooms brought the occupancy up to 5 rooms. Although the Colonel offered a free mixed drink at the bar but Ben declined. He was tired and wanted to check in with Fran and Ann.

The room was tired and grey but still clean. He made the tougher call first, lucky for him no one answered: "Hey Sissy, we're in Van Horn. Texas about 75 miles from El Paso. The Caddy's radiator gave out and we are getting it replaced tomorrow. We are staying at the almost world famous El Mountain Hotel. We're fine and hope Theo is doing better. I'll call you from the road after we get the car fixed."

Now if Ben had said there was no need to call him back, Fran, a well-established older sister, would have thought she needed to call him back right away.

He laid down for a nap. These naps after or during a long day were getting habit forming. They were that enjoyable. Not as enjoyable as connecting with Ann, but not half bad. Ben planned on improving his nap taking ability with practice. He had promised to meet Don for dinner at 7 pm. Don, of course, was taking the colonel up on the free drink and said he would be thinking about appetizers, not free.

But just as he was about to close his eyes, he heard a POP and then his favorite voice: "Boy, I know someone who's had another challenging day, how did it go?"

"Long and difficult. Don's been ok but doesn't say much, there's something on his mind."

"Is it his job?"

"Nooo, he lost his job but that's not unsual for him. I don't think that's all there is to it."

"What about the home front?"

"It probably would have been better to be upfront with his wife about the job loss but they seem to be as close as ever." That couple really did have a strong positive connection. They used to talk at least once a day but now, it was a never ending texting session.

"Wonder what's going on, is he sick? Something serious?"

"If the amount of BBQ has anything to do with it, maybe. His intake has been amazing. But no, I don't think that's it."

"We all go through tough times when we grow weary, look at what happened to you after I died…I felt so bad."

"Hey we're both, especially you, in a better place now. It's great being able to talk to you now."

"Ben, would you feel this same way if we weren't talking but you were simply imagining it?"

"What are you saying, like what my shrink said? A hallucination?"

"No I'm just thinking outside the box.. With a hallucination, you could see me and hear me anytime you wanted. You could even have dreams."

"Dreams and memories, I got plenty. It's the real Ann I want, not an imagined one."

"What's the difference?"

"Everything, I think,,"

"Ok, just wondering. Gotta go." POP. And she was gone.

But Ben was not. Wondering what Ann had meant or was hinting at, Ben couldn't say. As a result, he couldn't nap. Was Ann saying she wasn't real? Or was she suggesting, he'd be better off with a hallucination or as Ann liked to put it: a free ranging thought. In any case, what was she saying? Why would she even say that? Was she even real? Ben needed time to process this. He wished there was someone he could talk to-like a professional counselor who wasn't afraid to deal with Spirits. They must have lots of those in Sedona. Ben thought about it some more. He wished Ann had talked to him more before he talked to Fran, Esther and Larry. Especially, Larry. In addition, he still hadn't talked to Sue. How was he going to handle this? What would Ben do, next time Ann popped in? What could he say? Was he crazy? Were the doctors right? What difference would THAT make?

Ben sat in the room and watched a tumble weed roll by. He sat for a while and let his mind meander. He listened to the faucet drip in the bathroom. Drip... Drip... For some reason, he wasn't sure why, he felt it symbolized the time in Ben's life passing. Drip... Drip... He wasn't ready to let go of this life when there was so much to see and feel. Ben wanted to watch their kids continue to mature. He didn't want to miss the payback of watching them deal with teenagers of their own. He still wanted to see, hear and taste what the world offered every day, and to the extent he could, especially with Ann. Did it matter if Ann was real or a figment of his imagination? What's the difference? Did he really care? Not, too much to Ben's thinking now that he thought about it. Ben would prefer a real Ann as opposed to an imaginary one. He carried her permanently on the inside of his heart. But he loved her either way, real or not, and didn't want to waste any more of his time/life with Ann pondering over it, too much. It was already 7:10 pm. Time to get down to the dining room.

CHAPTER 16

TASTING ANOTHER'S LIFE

Ben went down and saw Don at a large table with 5 people leaving one empty chair for him. They were knee deep in appetizers. Peanut shells, really. They were spread all over the floor and that was just one of the perks, when you owned the joint. There were about 10 bottles of Shiner Boch Beer on the table. 3 were unopened. Ben grabbed an unopened one and joined the party. Besides Don, the Colonel, his wife Lorita who insisted on being called the Boss, her daughter Juanita, who took the chair closest to the kitchen, and Terry, of course, who was now wearing a straw cowboy hat but otherwise was dressed the same.

"Welcome, stranger, welcome!" bellowed Don, "We were just having an interesting conversation on what makes Texas so unique." Needless to say, Don was wearing a cowboy hat, too.

"Fascinating. Don, how long have you been down here?"

"About 3 beers, I mean 3 hours." Don chuckled. The Colonel went back to expounding on what made Texas unique: "So because Texas fought for its independence from Mexico and was an independent country for close to

10 years, we have independent DNA baked or should I admit brewed, in our jeans." Ben was hopeful, he meant genes.

Don had a questioning that was buzzing around his head: "Why do you think it's so different than the American Patriots who fought the British in the American Revolution?"

"Ah, you Anglos don't understand. We have been here for over 500 years and our state was created in perpetual conflict. We start off with the fall of the Great Aztec Empire. Then the Spanish Colonial Empire. Next Texas and her struggles against Mexico, followed by the American Civil War. Remember through this whole time, Spanish has been the primary language here for those 500 years. The passion and expression of that language has influenced everyone in the state including native born Texas Anglos like Terry."

Ben was still only on his 1st beer but the Colonel's civics lesson was somehow making sense. Texas was unique, mostly, because the people there believed they were-unique. Interesting.

"So Lorita, how did you meet the history professor?"

"We both grew up in the area and we met in junior high. We got married right before he signed up for the air force so he could get an education and we could see the world.. My family has been here almost 400 years. It was time for a change."

"How much change was it?" Don was curious, too.

"A lot for this area, you betcha. But I already had my required 20 years in and we just wanted to end up home. We had been stationed in New Jersey,

Hawaii, Guam, Kuwait, Greenland, Germany and South Carolina. We couldn't handle the BBQ and Mexican food there so when he retired, we came home. A few years later, we saw El Mountaine was for sale so we took a gamble and bought it."

"How has it worked out for you?"

"We've never been happier, losing money. I keep busy and the Colonel can manage the lobby. "

Lorita left to check on the Baked Pistachio Chicken. She came back a few minutes later; "Almost done."

"How 'bout you, Juanita, what brought you back?"

Ben was fascinated by people's stories. How did they end up where they were? Why did they take one fork in the road? Did they even see the fork? Did they give these decisions much thought? Ben believed everyone had an interesting story- some were just tougher to unearth. Some people never wanted to look back. For others, that's all they could do- a never ending repeat cycle of discussing the good old days.

Juanita sighed, looked down and then smiled at her husband Terry: "I had been working in Dallas as a supervisor in a call center while my first husband was managing a shoe store. This was after I had attended the CIA."

"Really? You were a spy?"

"Nah, the CIA stands for the Culinary Institute of America where I trained to be a Chef." It was tough getting by even on 2 incomes and then we had twins: Lisa and Becky. I couldn't handle the pay, hours and nights as a beginning Chef so I took a gig that worked better. Then I discovered Mark, a shoe store manager, couldn't manage to keep it in his pants around the customers. (He wasn't just helping female customers try on the shoes.) After the second time, I decided to leave him. I decided to regroup back here and the day I drove back, my car broke down and I met Terry. The rest is history." Ben could see why Terry went for Juanita –her eyes sparkled when she talked about the twins or Terry.

"Ok, Terry, you're next. Open up.."

"There isn't much to say other than I am the luckiest guy in Van Horn after meeting Juanita. I had been working as a mechanic for a Chevy dealer in El Paso when my uncle died and left me this gem, his combined junkyard and towing service."

"Sounds interesting to me."

Yeah but what about you two desperadoes? You two are the most interesting characters we've had this way since Willie Nelson and Fiona Apple each got stopped for suspected criminal smoking activity on I-10."

Just then Juanita walked back in with the peppery chicken encrusted with pistachios. She served it with home grown cooked vegetables. It smelled delicious and tasted even better. Don said it was as good as the best BBQ, he had so far on the trip. From Don that was high praise, indeed. Ben hoped that Ann could somehow smell it. For dessert, there was fresh coffee and strawberry pie.

But Terry was determined to find out what brought those strangers out to this obscure part of the prairie:

"So fess up, how did you end up here?"

Ben answered vaguely: "It's been a while since we had a road trip."

Don thought he had a better answer: "We are on a Beef BBQ tour of the Southwest."

"You ain't really on the lam from the authorities?"

Don turned grey and looked around the room: "Why are you saying that?"

Terry notice the strange look on Don's face. Ben noticed it, too. Terry thought he would try to set him at ease: "Hey, It's not as if you robbed a bank."

Don choked on his drink, Ben got a sinking feeling. Don had worked for a bank. Yep, there was something more, going on there. But Ben didn't see Don as someone who would steal for himself. He just wasn't the type.

Don said he was beat and after carefully looking around the dining area, quickly went to his room. Ben was curious as to what there was to do in Van Horn, Texas if you didn't have a car.

Terry said Van Horn was chockful of fun things to do including Tumbleweed Mini Golf and The Texas Mountain Trail. He offered to lend them his prized first car, a 1984 Chevy Citation so they could take a drive and go hiking. Terry told him, it was the first car he ever owned. Before heading off to bed, Ben thanked him and made arrangements to walk over and pick up the Citation tomorrow.

Ben fell asleep with his clothes on, listening to the ESPN Game of the Week. He was still wearing them when Ann woke him up at 6 am: "Come on, Benny, it's time to rise and shine."

"Hey Ann, good to hear from you, what time is it?"

"Like I said, it's time to get up. Want some coffee? Gonna have to make it yourself unless you want some virtual instant coffee."

"That sounds great. (Ben wasn't awake enough yet to realize she was kidding about the virtual coffee.) It was a long day. Did you stop by?"

"Yeah but you were in a deep sleep. Wasn't sure when or if you would wake up."

"No kidding. I woke up and wasn't sure where I was at first." Ben hated that feeling.

"So how much further do you expect to get today?"

"Our initial plan was to spend the night in El Paso but the Caddy broke down and it's getting fixed today."

"So what are you are going to do?"

"Not really sure. The repairman offered me the use of a Chevy Citation. Can't turn down that chance"

"Wait a minute, wasn't that the crappy car your Dad used to drive?"

"You've got a good memory. That 1984 Citation was the worst car, my Dad ever owned. I remember once the hatch lock broke off when I drove it"

Ann laughed: "I remembered that when your Dad tried to give it to you, you replied that he would have to pay you to take it."

"Yes I remembered that when Terry the repair man offered me his car. I didn't have the heart to turn him down, it was his first car and he had fond memories of them. I sure didn't."

"So when are you heading out today?"

"After breakfast tomorrow, after the car is repaired."

"I'll catch you later." POP.

Ben walked downstairs and into the dining room for breakfast. Don was nibbling on some bacon. He also had a Spicy Mexican Breakfast Pastry. These pastries did not use typical American sugar. Mexican sugar was less refined and more authentic. There were no eggs to go with it. The Colonel didn't believe in eggs and he was in charge of breakfast. His daughter was still at her home, helping to get her family going that day. Patrons in need of protein could have breakfast tacos, oatmeal, bacon or bean burritos with salsa. But no eggs. The Colonel was allergic to them, anyways.

Don liked Ben's idea of a country drive, followed by a hike in the hills. But he was still insistent on stopping in Juarez for a visit. Don said it was because he hadn't been out of the country in a while but Ben wasn't sure. Don was getting more mysterious as the trip was going on. He had even brought his duffle bag downstairs at breakfast. When questioned, he became defensive about it, saying he just felt safer having his stuff with him. Ben and Ann both thought it strange, but then again some famous writer once said: as people age, they don't change- they just become more concentrated versions of themselves. True enough.

Then again, Don had been acting strange (even for him) throughout the trip. From the start, Don was in an immediate need to get out of town. A real hurry like the 5 year old boy who can't wait for the bathroom any longer. Then there was the constant looking over his shoulder and Ben's too, for that matter. It was almost as if he was expecting to get tapped on his shoulder by law enforcement at any moment.

Then there was the weird money deal. Don had used cash to pay for everything on the trip. Everything. It was as if, he didn't want to leave a paper trail. But his wallet was so thick with 20's and 50's that Ben thought he would fall over when he sat on a chair. Then again, Don always had been a little unbalanced.

But the county highways near the hiking trails were everything you would want on a road trip. They were curvy, scenic with the hills on one side (generally) and not another car in sight. They pulled off into a parking area and began to climb. It was a lot more challenging and hills seemed to have grown now that they were hiking. The dry dirt smelled good in an earthy way. In Texas, even the dirt smelled better, Ben thought. Or, at least, that's what Frannie would say.

"So Don, why the strong urge to go to Juarez?"

"No particular reason. I've just never been there. I know lots of people who retired or started over in Mexico."

"Are you thinking of "starting over" in Mexico? What's going on? Seriously."

"Nope. Nothing is going on." That wasn't true but even after 1357 miles, Don still wasn't willing to lay his cards on the table. He couldn't. Don had an important meeting in Mexico and he thought it was better and safer that Ben didn't know about it. We all try to keep our secrets, well, secret. It is often said that telling a secret to another person, is one too many. True enough, Don thought.

They hiked, mostly in silence, for about another hour. Then Don through Google directed him to another BBQ, in a different town but yet again in a converted gas station. Why do so many BBQ joints end up in old gas stations? But it was good, really good. Both had the Man Handler Lunch Special: 2 beef ribs, burnt ends, potato salad AND coleslaw. Ben was stuffed and felt he had a not so benign BBQ tumor growing in his stomach. After stopping at Terry's who said he would drop the Caddy off later this afternoon, they went back to the motel to poop and nap. After all, their bodies were signaling that they were middle aged. They had to respect their colons.

Later that afternoon, they shared a couple of Mondelo Beers with Terry and the colonel. With it being so tough to scratch out a living in this part of the state, Ben wanted to get a better understanding of what tied the residents here and why it wouldn't let them go.

The Colonel belched and then expressed his thoughts: "My family has been here for over 300 years. There is something in the dirt that my nose needs to smell every day. It is the opposite of an allergy, it is a daily necessity"

"But couldn't you just learn to be somewhere else, do something else?"

"Ah, but as a short timer Anglo, you wouldn't understand." The Colonel smiled in his personal recognition of the knowledge, he was about impart: "We are Tejanos, not just Texans. We are descendants of the original settlers of Tejas, when it was part of the great Mexican State, long before there was any Texas. My family goes back hundreds of years. My great, great, great grandparents and their ancestors are buried here at St. Domingo's. Someday, I will join them in the same cemetery. Eventually, our children and their children will be buried there, too."

Ben began to realize, it was this blood pledge of continuity to his ancestors that kept the Colonel and his family here. Maybe that explained why so many other Americans were anxious and unsettled. They kept moving and rambling to new places, searching, yearning for a place to finally call home. But they still had no sense of time and place of the land that they temporarily inhabited.

Or maybe, the Colonel had it all or at least partially wrong, some people need to ramble, always trying something new. Maybe that was built into their DNA. The 3 of them, Ben, Don and the Colonel went outside to smoke some Swisher Sweet Cigars. They could hear the Zarcadias bugs chirp loudly. They watched some fire flies float by in group formation. They each pondered on what the other said. Everyone has their own truth. Not all of them face it.

CHAPTER 17

Proper Boundaries

The next day after a proper breakfast that included eggs, as per practice, the Colonel wasn't cooking, they said their goodbyes and checked out. The Caddy was ready and washed, waiting in front of the hotel just like Terry promised. In fact, the keys were in the ignition, it being small town Texas where everybody knew each other and their cars. They were only about 50 miles from El Paso. El Paso is a large sprawling city with 800,000 residents. Its far older and larger sibling Juarez is just across the Rio Grande River which is the international border between Mexico and the United States. The cities are basically one large metropolitan area with several million people. United by business and families but divided by current political interests, Juarez had in particular grown in response to the U.S. Mexico Free Trade Agreement. While El Paso was fairly safe with 23 murders in 2018, Juarez was held hostage by the drug trade with approximately 1500 murders there that year alone.

Ann had been very much against them going to Juarez when they talked in the morning: "It's not safe, for either of you to go there."

"But I promised Don that I would go. I don't want him to think that I'm chicken."

"That is one of the dumbest things I have ever heard a male say. You think your testosterone will be adversely affected if you make the smarter decision not to go. It's not a sightseeing trip, it's a war zone in Juarez and you two middle aged Anglos would be a prime kidnapping target."

"We'll be careful." Besides, Ben believed that it might help him finally figure out what Don was really up to. Something was wrong. Seriously wrong. As a long term friend, Ben felt he had a duty, as silly as that sounded, to try and help Don.

"It's not Don, I'm worried about. He already, nearly killed both of you with trying to grab the steering wheel. Isn't that enough danger for one trip?" Ann was not impressed with the male logic behind looking for trouble and never chickening out when it would be the responsible thing to do.

"He was just kidding, he wasn't serious."

"An accident would have been deadly serious and I am not going to be part of it." With that, Ann POPPED off in a huff.

It being 10 am, their first stop in El Paso was the Lucchese Cowboy Boot Factory Outlet store not too far from the airport. If Ben was going to try wearing cowboy boots again, he didn't want to make the same mistake as before. If you wondered why cowboys walked funny, it's because they are walking on their heels. While cowboy boots were often hand tooled pieces of art, the last time Ben found a cheap pair, he also received a nasty case of planter fasciitis on his heels which he and his feet found extraordinarily painful. Here in the store connected with the factory, Ben bought a beautiful pair of black cherry leather boots with a side zipper for only $600. Other boots ranged from $200 to $3000 a pair. The sales consultant assured him these boots would not bring a return of the previous foot condition that felt like needles being stuck in his heels. Don, of course, already had a decent pair of cowboy boots but bought another pair made out of Ostrich leather anyways and still wanted to get to Juarez before 1 pm.

So following the Lucchese stop, they decided to park near the international crossing (US side) and walk across the border, instead of driving, so as to avoid a lengthy car search looking for drugs on the way out and in. There was also little sense in driving a car with Minnesota license plates unless one was trying to get purposely kidnapped. Don had heard of a particular, recommended, Italian restaurant in a major hotel, where Ben could wait safely while Don ran his errands. The errands still allegedly consisted of hitting a pharmacy for some much cheaper version of a thyroid medication he was taking. They grabbed a cab and after declining some proffered female companionship, they were dropped off at the hotel. The food was grand and the service impeccable but Ben tried to avoid looking at any of the steely eyed young or the hulking chunks protecting them. Weapons were only semi-concealed.

Then Don got up suddenly said he would cover the meal and would meet him at the hotel bar in an hour-hour and half. Just like that he was gone. Ben waited 30 seconds and then followed him, determined to find out something. He jumped when he heard a gentle POP behind him, then relaxed when he realized it was only Ann: "Did you really think, I was going to let you walk into this mess alone?" Ben was grateful but being a guy, pretended to be miffed: "What are you, my guardian angel?"

"Someone has to be. Always have. Always will."

He hurried up to try and keep within 200 feet of Don. But he was gone. Ben had put on his sunglasses so he wouldn't look so much like an available Anglo kidnap victim. Of course, the Lucchese Boots, made in America, the free Lucchese baseball hat he was wearing, didn't help matters any. "Did you see where he went?" Downtown Juarez was a bustling place.

Ann thankfully had been keeping her eyes (such as they were) on the prize: "I just saw him walk into an sleek one story building with guards in the front." Ben looked. The building had a small sign: Ricardo Breamo, Abogado. This made no sense. Why would Don be meeting a Mexican attorney? Why would he lie about it? Most importantly, why would the attorney need guards in from of his office? Ben decided to ask Ann for a favor, a big one: "Ann, could you please spiritize (he still didn't know what to call it) in there and check out what's going on?"

"Wish I could but I can't. We Spirits, all have to do a monthly activity sheet on our comings and goings. Like attorneys, we can fudge a little on our time but this is way off the reservation or should I say nation? I just don't want to risk what you and I have."

Ben pressed a little: "Come on, 5-10 minutes tops. It's not like I'm asking you to do something improper. This is our friend Don."

| 119

"Are you kidding me?" Even Spirits can get shrill: "This is obviously a drug dealer attorney, there's no way I could explain that to the Big Cheese." Maybe the person in charge of the universe, He/She/They were probably from Wisconsin. That would explain a lot of improbable Packer victories. But Ann would not budge. So Ben and Ann walked back to the hotel where Ann felt it was safer for him to wait. Don came back an hour later, looking flustered and carrying a small white Farmacia (Pharmacy) bag.

Ben went first: "How did it go at the pharmacy?"

"Oh, that was a 20 minute wait in line and then another 45 minutes to get the medication. 1/3 of the cost than in the US. Same drug, same dosage. I went to a reputable place."

"Stop anywhere else while you were gone?" Ben wanted to hear how Don would answer.

Don lied: "No, why do you ask?"

Ben was angry: "Because maybe, you just plain forgot about the meeting you just had at a drug dealer attorney's office who had security guards with Uzi machine guns in the front."

Don: "Were you spying on me? Well for your information, maybe, just maybe, I was looking into how to buy a retirement home here."

"Are you kidding here? These are serious drug people, you shouldn't be involved with them."

"I am not involved in drugs, I swear."

"Then, what is it?"

"Trust me, you don't want to know and I don't want to tell."

"Don, we're good friends…"

"Please just leave it alone. For both our sakes.."

Ben had a very uncomfortable feeling.

Chapter 18

Be Careful What You Ask For...

Don and Ben went back to the U.S. soon after. They took a cab from the hotel to the border and went through US Customs. Don didn't want to get caught bringing in so many thyroid prescription pills(That's what Don said they were, now Ben didn't know whether to believe him) and wanted to split the pills between the two of them, to lessen his potential criminal liability for improper medication importation. Ben was still angry and refused his friend's bidding even though many U.S. citizens did the same thing to escape high U.S. pharmaceutical prices. That was maybe, a good thing about guys, when they were angry at someone, even a longtime friend, they would often times stew silently, rather than openly deal with their feelings. Then again, you couldn't know what they were thinking. Ultimately the drugs were not an issue, as middle aged Anglos, they were waved through. When they got to Ben's car, they needed to talk about where they were going next. It was already 3 pm.

Ben figured they could make it to Tucson for the night in 4 1/2 hours, or Phoenix in 6 ½ hours. From Phoenix it was only 2 more hours to Sedona but

Ben did not like making that drive at night. Besides it was dang pretty driving through the stunning Verde Valley to even more gorgeous Red Rock Country in the day time. First though they had to get a couple of things settled.

"When were you going to tell me about the meeting with the Attorney in Juarez?"

"To be honest? Hopefully, never. I'm sorry I couldn't tell you. I still can't talk about it. Someday I will when I can, I promise."

"You gotta tell me now, you're not carrying anything illegal?"

"Except for the thyroid medication, no."

"Ok, now are you involved in something like a criminal conspiracy?"

Don thought for a moment then "No" He said slowly like he was breathing it out.

"All right, what haven't you told me?"

"I can't. If I did speak about it to another person then according to my attorney it would be a conspiracy and I am not sucking you into this."

"That sounds ominous."

"It is, can we talk about something else?"

"Sure, as long as you can tell me you're safe now and you'll let me know when you're not." It's what you do for friends. You look out for each other

"Deal. We're safe now and I promise I'll let you know when you're not." It was only after the whole thing ended, that he realized that Don had not made the promise on keeping the two of them safe. That Don had made no such promise about his own safety.

They decided to just drive on Highway I-10W til they got tired. The miles rolled along. First, Las Cruces, New Mexico and then another hour to Deming, which was the county seat of Luna County. Then one more hour to Lordsburg, New Mexico.

They stopped for a quick dinner here because it was already 5:30 pm and Don believed in always searching for a hamburger believed that would find flavor in the eyes of the Lord. When they stopped at a nondescript diner off the highway, Ben looked up the town in Google.

Even though, Lordsburg was the county seat of Hidalgo County, like many parts of rural southwest, its population was falling. Quickly. In 2000, it was 3400 residents, down to 2800 in 2010 and only 2400 now. The future looked tough. Some hardy people were trying to start some sort of development. Ben learned that the city was originally founded as a railroad town, but during World War Two, the US operated an internment camp there for 1500 Japanese Americans Citizens. Unbelievable, what people could do to their neighbors, their friends all in the name of alleged patriotism which masked underlying racism. Still, though for film buffs, who had little or no knowledge of the camps, the city still had an allure for being the last stop in the famous movie: Stagecoach. Ben felt something threatening in the diner where no one spoke. Every one's eyes looked angry and darted back and forth. Several patrons wore large handguns openly and others surely had them concealed. Even the burger tasted menacing.

Ben asked Don, if he had the same uncomfortable feeling in the diner, once they were safely out on the Interstate: "Did you feel something strange in the diner, too?"

"A little gas but nothing extraordinary or paranormal, why?" UFO and paranormal activity was big in the Southwest. Out here, there was a lot of space on the land and in people's minds for aliens to land.

"It felt just felt creepy to me, that's all."

"Creepy is, as creepy feels." Don didn't feel it at all and was not sympathetic, in the least. Maybe, he was still pissed over Ben tailing him in Juarez.

Ben shook his head and the odd feelings lessened, the further they drove from the town. Ben was not a superstitious man, but he believed they had just traveled through an unhappy zone, where past lives silently cried out their anguish and pain from the injustice our country committed against our own citizens.

While it was only 75 miles from Lordsburg to Wilcox, Arizona, there weren't any towns in between. While retirees and young professionals were flocking to the big and medium sized cities of the southwest, the small rural centers were literally dying off. It was as if the towns had an invisible sign that read: Welcome to (Fill in the Blank), where dreams come to die. That was harsh but accurate. Sometimes a person needed to just pick up and leave.

Both of them wanted to keep on driving when they reached Wilcox. Neither was still talking much because of what had happened in Juarez, Mexico. Sometimes, a friendship takes a dramatic and unhappy turn.

It would have been nice to stop at the Saguaro National Park (East entrance) where hundreds, no thousands of Saguaros soared 40 feet in the sky but since it was dark now there was nothing to see. The Saguaros lived up to several hundred years old and bloomed sometime during March or April.

Benson, too would have been fun as a jumping off point to Tombstone or the remarkable Kartchner Underground Caverns.

Tombstone, although small, only 1300 population had a hallowed spot in the history of the Wild West. Home of the OK Corral where Doc Holiday, Wyatt Earp and his brother took out the bad guys in daily reenactments, and Boot Hill cemetery where outlaws and locals are buried.

Kartchner Caverns, an Arizona State Park is not as well-known but endlessly fascinating. Seeing stalagmites, stalactites, and strange formations almost as if it was a movie set for the planet Mars.

But the 58 year old Boys were tired and just kept driving. They weren't in a rush but just wanted to get where they were going. They eventually reached Tucson which was less than 1 1/2 hours from Phoenix. When they saw a Super 8 hotel, they decided to quit for the night and pulled in. Before walking into his room, Don said he was sorry.

"For what?" Ben still wanted to know.

"For everything. Don't think, I don't appreciate what you tried to do for me because I do.." With that Don lifted up his suitcase and closed the door to his room.

Ben stood in the hallway for a minute and then shook his head. That was strange. He was too tired to wonder what Don meant. Ben walked into the room and loosened his Agate Bolo that he bought for $10 allegedly 50% off, at an El Paso gas station. He found the Rand Mc Nally Map of the US folded in his back pocket all day. He looked at it and realized he had folded it wrong.

He was too tired to fix it now, so he just tossed across to the other bed. But it strangely didn't land and instead started floating around the room. Either, he was really tired (maybe even asleep) or Ann was messing with him. It was the latter.

POP. Ann appeared in a cowgirl shirt, short skirt made from jean material and red cherry cow girl boots. Even with the cowgirl straw hat, she looked mighty fine for a cowgirl Spirit.

"Hey Annie Oakley, how is it going? You're looking good."

Never try and sweet talk an angry cowgirl: "Don't waste your time trying to hit on me. I know how good I look in this outfit. You're lucky, I didn't kill you for that stunt in Juarez."

"Hey, I knew I could manage the situation and protect Don."

'You could have been kidnapped or killed! Be honest, you still don't know what HIS situation is."

"Hey! I watched the movie Tombstone 3 times, I was ready."

"Can you just save that fake machismo stuff for your obituary notice after your death and not before?"

"What difference does it make?"

"Because your life is checked out under my name in the celestial library, I'm responsible for you being returned to the right spot at the right time."

"Isn't that romantic"

"It is, what it is."

"What does that, mean?"

"Not sure, just always wanted to use it in a dramatic scene."

"And so you have…"

Can we PLEASE talk about this tomorrow when I'm more awake?"

"Fine but then, I'm not sleeping with you, tonight."

"That's OK as long as I get some sleep."

"Hrump! Good night! POP."

That night, Ben began his sleeping, with the uncomfortable rest of the seriously stewed.

CHAPTER 19

THE END OF THE BEGINNING

Their last day started like many others. After Ann returned later, when they both had cooled down, Ben had spent much of the night talking with her. They never ran out of things to talk about. But when he woke up, she was gone. Ben knew he was a deep sleeper and like Ann said: "why waste energy on a sleepy head?" Ben looked forward to talking to her later that day. Indeed, firing that shrink was the healthiest thing, he ever did.

Surprisingly, Don was already out at his car with his bag, when Ben arrived. Don seemed anxious about something and eager to go. They were both ready to leave Tucson in their rearview mirror. They gassed up and then went through the drive through for breakfast before getting back on I-10 for the short drive to Phoenix before heading up to the Red Rocks of Sedona.

Looking back later, Ben would always remember that day as another cloudless day but one that had blue skies that were magnetic to his eyes. Inviting. Piercing. But after about 20 minutes of driving, they saw a road block ahead and flashing police lights, looking like a sideways Christmas tree.

"That's strange… "Ben said "I thought the immigration road blocks were closer to the border. (They were about 60 miles away.) Wonder what's going on?"

"It's probably for me" said Don, slumping in his seat.

"Right, there's probably a FBI wanted poster of you for bank robbery." Ben was laughing, but stopped when he noticed Don wasn't, and had a strong twitch going on the left side of his face.

"There might be…" Don looked away far into distance. It was finally time to fess up.

Ben was beginning to feel uncomfortable as the road block drew closer. He could see police officers standing next to their cars that were blocking the highway. He cleared his voice: "What's going on?"

Don wouldn't look at him: "My misunderstanding of the Bank's refunding policy may have been intentional."

"That's crap and makes no sense. What did you do?" Ben started easing on the brakes there were now only 2 cars waiting in front of them.

"Well, you know that a few banks have been ripping off customers forever and I was in charge of monitoring suspicious activities. That gave me a lot of power in the Ethernet Lands. I may have decided to even the score for some people."

"How many is some?"

"2,257 customers to be precise."

"How did you find the people?"

"Well, I started with a simple algorithm that predicted what customers were most likely ripped off and then I would search their files to determine if it occurred. But there were too many individuals to keep track of and I realized those unauthorized entries would be alerting the bank at some point so I didn't have a lot of time. He smiled sheepishly and then continued:

"So I designed my own stealth computer program that looked for Gopher State National Bank customers who paid the most service fees and had the lowest income based on their credit scores. I paid them back with a little bonus." Like Ben always thought, Don was a genius with that computer junk as he called it.

"How much?"

"A big 10." Don smirked. No good usually, ever came from what was behind that smirk. Ben knew from experience. Except for maybe this time.

"10,000 dollars?" Ben was incredulous. "Maybe, I can help?" Ben had savings.

"10 million dollars in total.." The number hung in the air.

"No, really." That couldn't be right. Don would never be that stupid.

"Yes, really…You got to understand, to Gopher State National Bank, this is a rounding issue less than what they pay the CEO in 6 months as a bonus. These corporate bottom feeders won't stop til we make them."

Don was serious but if true, he would be going to jail. For a long time. Only the little guys actually did the time, CEO's almost never. Another car was being let through the road block. Ben wondered what would happen to Don and much more urgently, what was going to happen to him? Were the Cops going to consider him, an accomplice subject to charges? Could Don get off on some technicality? An Insanity Plea? Don seemed pretty certain of what he was doing.

Don looked at Ben and said: "Don't worry, I ordered this shit sandwich and I'm going to eat it, all on my own. I'm not going to drag you into it. You didn't know. You're safe."

"But what about you?"

"I'll be fine.."

"No you won't! Prison ain't no Herzl Summer Youth Camp. Does Deb know about this?"

"Of course not. Truthfully, she'll probably be relieved. She won't have to clean up for me anymore and she'll be free."

"Hey, she's never gonna give up on you- you stupid lug nut. She loves you, God knows why. But what about us? Who's gonna go out on those road trips and sleazy restaurants with me?"

"I'm not stupid. You're not on your own. I heard you talking with Ann in the Motel Drek last night. Those motel walls have less sound insulation than a rice cake. I couldn't hear her, only heard you. But she's here somehow, isn't she?"

"Yep. I don't exactly understand it either, but it works." The car in front of them was let through the road block. It was their turn. Ben could see the cops tense up and put their hands closer to their holsters. They knew.

Ben turned to Don: "I gotta know, is this why you were in such a hurry to go on this trip? Or were you really that worried about me? As your best friend, I'm interested in knowing."

"It was both, to be truthful. Gopher was closing in and Deb suspected something wrong was going on. I wanted an off ramp, in case I chickened out of doing the Abbie Hoffman thing in the courtroom, when it was time to fess to up to my and Gopher's responsibility for the economic crimes against the poor of this country. Besides, I thought you really needed an adventure trip. Looks like we both got one. Tell Ann, I'm glad you're back together and at least Deb will know where she can find me for the next 15-20 years."

"Take care of yourself. Maybe we can hit Embers when you get out."

Their car inched up, it was their turn. Ben put the car windows down, when asked, and they both put their hands on the dashboard. The policeman leaned over and smiled: "Well hello there, we've been looking for you two. Would you step out of the car slowly, one at a time starting with Mr. Dodge?" Don got out and he was cuffed. Funny thing was, Don was still joking:

"Don't worry, I'm still gonna cover my share of the expenses."

"I'm not worried. I know where I can find you." This is how guys showed they cared, by joking.

Don was then handcuffed put into a Law Enforcement car. They pushed his head down as they placed Don in the back seat. He was still smiling as the police car took off.

Ben, on the other hand, was scared to death. After he got out of the car they did not cuff him but did place him in a squad car. Then they took down the road block and drove both to the local sheriff's office.

6 hours later, Don was booked and held without bail as a flight risk, while Ben was released on his own recognizance, as long as he agreed to surrender his passport, not to leave the country and to cooperate with the Federal Authorities.

Ben was dropped off at his car where Ann was waiting in a beautiful tan Stella Mc McCarthy pants suit that only he could see.

"Thanks for waiting."

"And risk missing the return of Donnie and Clyde? Not a chance. That Don is one in a million in a good way."

"You mean, ten million. Where to next, my Lady? The Winter or Summer Palace?"

"The Red Rocks of Sedona are calling. I haven't been there since before I died. You can't keep avoiding our place to avoid our memories. Gotta make some new ones. Let's go!" So they did.

END OF PART ONE

Part Two
Almost Home

Chapter 20

Then There Were Two. Sort Of.

So it was down to just the two of them when they left Tucson, as Don was being held in jail under no bail as a flight risk, pending trial. Ben had enjoyed checking out the history of the city which goes back thousands of years. The Hohokam Tribe had lived in the area from roughly 450 to 1450 AD. A Spanish Mission was started in 1700 AD and the City was now over 1 million people. But both Ben and Ann were eager to get up to Sedona and leave Tucson behind.

It wasn't far from Tucson to Phoenix on Highway I-10, a little more than 100 miles away. But when the dust storms came, it was if they have been dropped in the Sahara Desert. While there are signs warning of sudden wind storms, it did not do it justice. It was worse than a Minnesota snow storm. Even after the car in front of him put on their tail lights and Ben did the same, they still could not be seen. Ben pulled off the road but left the car on so the battery would not be drained. Then in 20 minutes, Poof! It was gone like it had to be somewhere else in a hurry. When all the cars pulled back onto the highway, Ben did the same.

Ann had stayed with him, the entire time. Ben really appreciated that but still wished he could have held her hand:

"Boy that was something I hope I never see again. It was like a blizzard made of sand." Ben shivered. He had been through more than enough Minnesota Snow Storms but this was worse. Far worse:

"I wasn't sure we were going to make it."

"Well, we did and we're ok, that's what is important."

"Even if we crashed, you couldn't be hurt anyways, right?" Ben wanted reassurance. He still wasn't clear how this spiritual energy always worked,

"As long as I'm not hit by a Solar Storm or I don't get sucked into a Black Hole, I should be ok. Although lightening can cause serious damage to a virtual outfit. Like Mom always said, it never pays, to dress up on a travel day."

"Well, I'm really glad you're ok- thanks for sticking around. For a minute or two, I thought the car might flip and that would be it."

"Hey cowboy, you got more than a few rodeos left to ride in."

"While I appreciate the sentiment, there are no guarantees. Look at you for example. One day you're here, the next you're dead."

"You sure know how to charm the ladies! I'm still here. But what about you? Where do you figure you'll finally end up when you go?"

"I wish we could go ahead with our original plan. Our ashes being dumped on the shores of Lake Superior like that friend of Joy's. But we did promise Esther we'd be buried in a cemetery."

"Are you still going to insist on the granite checkerboard seat near our plot?"

"Oh, I don't know. I just wasn't born with the G gene."

"G gene?"

""You know, with a belief in God or Goddess or some unifying force that governs and regulates the universe. It's just missing in me. Must be a production flaw."

"I don't believe that- you're one of the most thoughtful, generous persons I know. You believe in giving. It's just a different kind of religious belief. You believe in the inherent goodness of people. Admit it, you've always been spiritual, just in a different way, like in your love of nature, too."

"So what about you? Leaving aside your current work on Spiritual Airlines."

"You know I've always been a spiritual person well before I died. I always found communal prayer helpful, I feel something when I pray with other people. It's like our personal prayers are amplified. Guess I was born with that God gene, kind of like, our daughter Esther."

"But don't you still believe before, in a life after death? Do you think that life force has to go somewhere?"

"Like we've talked about before, I believe we live on in the hearts and minds of people who love us."

"Ann, then you'll be living on for a very long time. Those grandkids adore you."

"Yeah, they are all pretty sweet."

"Speaking of food, wanna stop at the In and Out Burger in Phoenix on our way up to the hills?" Ben loved In and Out Burgers.

"That's not sweet."

"Yes but they have great Sweet Tea there."

"Whatever you want. Remember I don't eat any more.."

"Sorry, I forgot." That was true, Sometimes Ben would forget his wife Ann was dead when they were talking so intently. He figured it was a compliment to both of them. Alright, mostly her.

In and Out Burger was a long time hamburger sensation out west. Around for 50 years, they had an extremely limited menu but made them all extraordinarily well: Fresh Hamburgers, that you could order sloppy, hand peeled potatoes for fresh French fries daily and a condiments bar that included onions, pickles and pickled jalapenos. They also sold super T-shirts for $10. Ben usually liked to hit the joint that was located next to the Costco off the I-17 and Union Hills exit.

After a quick burger in his car, he wanted to keep talking to Ann and figured he couldn't do that either inside or outside the restaurant. He was getting tired of pretending to talk with her on his cell phone so he got take out. Ben was getting excited. They were finally getting closer to what they called their winter palace.

Once they passed the last planned community of Anthem where their Minnesota Snowbird friends Lisa and Frank lived year round, the suburbs dwindled quickly. Frank and Lisa had wisely retreated there from the snow years ago. Ben and Ann passed familiar signs warning them about forest fires and wandering Burros which their Republican friends made fun of as being Democrats.(The old Donkey and elephant symbols for the 2 political parties). They started climbing in the hills and leaving the Valley of the Sun.

Phoenix was hot, not just growth wise (The Chamber likes to brag that Phoenix is the fastest growing city in America.), but physically hot. It was common now for temperatures to hit 120 degrees Fahrenheit. Phoenix itself has over 100 days a year now where it hits at least 100 degrees. No amount of mist machines is going to cover up those high temperatures. That is serious heat and to beat it, people had to rise early or go outside after dusk.

When in Sedona, Ben and Ann tried to drive down to see the hot birds as they teased Lisa and Frank once a month. They were still great friends. Frank had been a political mentor to Ben and Ann adored Lisa. Sometimes they met less than half way at the Rock Spring Café where they served homemade pie in 27 flavors. They still had not convinced the contingent of other Minnesota Snowbirds to go there for pie, when they weren't busy sending "concerning" emails or texts to their Minnesota friends every time there was a serious snow storm. In recent years, these winter storms, seemed to be much more common.

Driving on Highway I-17 North, Ann and Ben barely noticed Black Canyon City. This was the end of the exurbs still connected to Phoenix. (An exurb according to geographers is technically a distant suburb). There was a BBQ joint that Don had always wanted to try called Chill and Grill Out. But it was going to be a long while before Ben thought Don would be out:

"You think Don will be ok in prison?"

"For Don, it should go just fine. We're talking federal prison here. He'll probably end up like Burt Lancaster in the movie: "Birdman of Alcatraz" and write a famous computer book or something."

"I sure hope so. Do you think you can POP in and see how things are going for him? He knows about us and is cool with it."

"Be a man and talk to him about his feelings yourself. Let him know about your concerns when he calls." Prisoners were not allowed cell phones in prison and were still limited to 2 calls a week.

"Will you please still look in on him, anyways?"

"I'll try but like I said, I'm limited to being heard or seen by one person at a time."

"You could at least check and make sure he is safe."

"Tell you what, let me talk to a more senior Spirit who has more experience- he or she or they might have an idea for a workaround. Besides, Don will be fine. Don will hopefully eat better and he won't keep those crazy hours. He'll finally get enough sleep. Did I ever tell you I actually looked at the Birdman's book called: Digest of Diseases of Birds? It was a remarkable ornithological book given that the author Robert Franklin Stroud wrote it in prison. He illustrated it, too. Sad that he died there after spending 54 years being incarcerated." Ann was smart, real smart.

Ben barely knew what ornithological meant (Study of Birds). Ann was smart enough to get admitted to medical school and brave enough to drop out when she realized that she liked examining books better than examining people. She had always considered a good book to be a good friend. Besides, she wanted enough time to have a real family and medical school with its long hours, was unforgiving. She didn't regret her choice and by becoming a librarian even if it was at United Healthcare of all places after a detour with the kids, she could share a love of books and research with many people.

They were traveling up higher now. Highway signs advised turning off air conditioning, to avoid straining car engines. Ben wasn't too worried about their Cadillac with its North Star engine. They passed Sunset Point Rest Stop and then Bloody Basin, where the US Army attacked a Native American encampment at dawn. The Army caused the death of up to 50 Native Americans, some of whom leaped to their death off the cliffs. While the Army believed they were attacking the Tonto Apache tribe that had earlier killed 3 settlers, some scholars now believe it was friendly Yavapai women and children who were caught up in the violence that early morning in 1873. Sadly, the Range Wars of the late 1860's and 1870's led to the death of many innocent victims. On both sides.

Right nearby was the Agua Fria (Cold water) National Monument which is located on a deep canyon created by the Agua Fria River which runs through it. While it was a relatively newly protected site, and doesn't draw many visitors, it has evidence of early inhabitation, including pictographs, petroglyphs and ancient ruins. Visitors hike down the canyon to the river and birders have observed over 150 different varieties of birds.

Next, they passed the exit for Arcosanti, which was and is a planned community that joins ecology and architecture into what its founder called arcology (Not a misspelling). Envisioned by the famed architect Palo Soleri, it has been still building for the last 50 years and his disciples support it by tours, workshops and casting bronze bells.

But they again did not stop and persisted, the silent siren of Sedona calling them. Still driving, climbing now on the edges of the magnificent Verde Valley, for a second they could see the famous Red Rocks in the distance. At times in the past, it had been a very treacherous trip for them in the rain, snow and dark even on I-17(old 89A from Prescott to Jerome portion would have been even worse). They passed Camp Verde where the Tonto Apaches were imprisoned and starved during the Range Wars. Today it's rumored for being where, Ted Williams' head is cryogenically frozen in a deep freeze. Someday, he could be brought back to life. (Ted Williams was one of the greatest baseball players ever, whose extraordinary eyesight, made him the last player to hit over 400 in 1941. He was also a fighter pilot during WW2 and the Korean War.) But they had keep moving. Their home, too, was calling, - no yelling for both of them.

CHAPTER 21

Returning

Next on Highway 17, they passed the Cliff Castle Casino on their right and the 260 exit for Cottonwood which called itself the Biggest Little City in America. Its population was only 12,000, but like many cities in Arizona, the city signs noted only their elevation and what year they were founded. Like Camp Verde, the population of Cottonwood had almost doubled in the last 10 years. Still, with its much more affordable housing and proximity to Sedona, many of the workers supporting the tourist and retiree population resided there.

Then suddenly, the highway sign announced it was only 2 miles for the exit to Highway 179 that would lead through Red Rock Country and on to Sedona. They were almost home-only 15 minutes away. If they had turned right, they would have been only 5 miles from Ben's favorite archeological site, The V Bar V Ranch with it its 1000 petroglyphs and astrological calendar. Even though Ben was a volunteer guide and it was open, there was no time or desire for a stop. Almost home.

They took a left, slipped underneath Highway 17 and continued west on 179. They were both quiet with anticipation. Then, around a curve to the right, there it was- the colorful sight that never ceased to amaze them.

The Red Rocks shining almost a Fall Maple Leaf Red. They were now 1 mile out away from the Village of Oak Creek which is where they lived. Oak Creek was technically a cooperative, not a village. The homeowners banded together to rescue the failed golf course/real estate development that was at the center of the Village in the 1970's. At the time, the homeowners set up the cooperative, the golf course was only days away from having its water turned off. It looked like a typical American suburb stuffed in the middle of a National Park. There were hiking trails and Red Rocks galore.

"Next to you, this is my favorite sight in the world." Ben meant that.

"You know, it does feel good to be back. It always does."

Ann and Ben talked about that quite a bit. There was something that just made them feel emotionally and physically better in Sedona. (Including the Village of Oak Creek where they lived.) They didn't know if it was the climate, the rocks or exercise, the trails, beautiful scenery or the unique and talented characters who were drawn there, but there was something special. Some people thought there were magnetic forces at work in the rocks that provided healing powers. More than a few believed in the powers of the Vortex which was allegedly an entry point to different dimensions. There were 5 so called Vortexes in Sedona, including Bell Rock less than a mile from their house. Bell Rock was literally next door to the Circle K convenience store. All Ben and Ann knew is that, there were a lot of crystals, rocks, gift shops, healers and tourists. (Averaging 3,000,000 visitors and growing each year.)

They took a left at Verde Valley School Road, drove past the only grocery store in town, and took a right on Bell Rock Boulevard. There they passed the Oak Creek Country golf club. (Some saw it as more a community senior center) that was designed by famed golfer Robert Trent Jones.

Ben and Ann liked to sneak on the golf course to stroll. Then it was just a left turn to their street. Green Golf Lane, not to be confused with Green Golf Drive. The street designers had been cursed with a stark lack of imagination when it came to street names, so as a result, there were many streets with similar names. They turned into their driveway and they were back. Home was an "A" frame, white stucco house surrounded by tall windows that overlooked Castle Rock. It was not a large home but the walls of glass made it Ann, Ben and their guests feel like they were still outside. Ben and Ann had been coming down for 20 years since Ann's friend Joy first invited them to visit. Later, Joy helped them find their present palace. There were still 3 heavy original white Adirondack chairs in the front and another covered outside seating patio area in the back. It was good to be home. It had been too long. On his own, Ben hadn't been able to face coming home, but with Ann alongside in whatever form she was, he was eager to get back. It was time.

CHAPTER 22

NOT QUITE PARADISE BUT CLOSE ENOUGH TO SPIT ON IT.

But Ann and Ben had not just come back to their house, they also had come back to their neighbors and friends. It was an unusual grouping of neighbors. In Sedona they usually were, but the neighbors were still their friends. Ben had not seen them since before Ann died, and Ben was now a marketable item as a widower. He would have been even more marketable if he had, a partial head of hair. Especially in a community that averaged over 65 years of age and was 60% female. Ben was determined to avoid any blue hair specials for now and besides, as an Official Dark Sky Community, there was no lighting at night anyways, outside of the main drag-179. In the village where they lived, there was little going on at night. He was not interested in venturing out at night anyways and he could make his own casseroles.

Their neighbors included Mary Jo who lived right behind them and was responsible for her personal nature park and saint statute collection. To the right, lived Steve and Lisa, who lived mostly on a diet of takeout food and Fox News. As long as they avoided politics, the two couples got along more than fine. Steve and Lisa had been two of their closest friends. Steve, too, was an archeology buff and passed on several monthly publications Ben's way. Lisa was an avid gardener and she understood the mysterious language of Plants. She could really talk to them and usually they responded. Lisa was up early, every day, tending to her garden and was a great resource. This being Arizona, there were very few grass yards but that did not mean there were not any plants including hardy native plants that residents considered weeds. Their neighbors to the left, were Sally and Rob, who were global climate transferees. After being washed out 3 times by gulf storms, they were determined to land in an area where hurricane meant a type of drink and not a repetitive risk with regular, massive cleanup obligations. It was unfortunate that their realtor had not warned them about the end of summer monsoon rain season.

Then there was Sid Fleshig who lived directly on the golf course. Sid was a successful realtor, who moved to Sedona after retiring from the army. He attributed his survival of 2 tours of duty in Iraq during heavy fighting, to a vial of magnetic meteorite dust on a necklace bought in Sedona. His mother, who lived in Glendale and dabbled in the mystic arts, sent it to Iraq to protect him. It worked. Sid visited Sedona on a leave home and caught a case of Red Rock Fever. He was enchanted with Sedona. Most Sundays, he could be found at Paul's Place in the Village, drinking beer, watching sports and trolling for potential clients.

Mary, across the street, was a gifted sculptor, who had a man's hands because prior to her sex change, she was Brad. She made extraordinary raw pieces of sculpture that were both primitive and sophisticated all at the same time. Everything just flowed in her work, and it was reminiscent of Alaskan Inuit Carving. Thankfully, she still enjoyed a belt of whiskey after finishing work. Many were the happy hour where the three of them watched the sun come down on Castle Rock which shined a glittering gold color for

5 to 10 minutes before turning a dull red as the Sun slipped away into the night.

Sometimes, there was a fourth person present, when Mary's daughter Glenna, a cookbook author, came down from Flagstaff. She was well known for being able to make vegan food taste interesting, not an easy skill.

Their final friends outside of the Temple bunch were Sally and Amy, a gay couple who owned a large successful natural foods mail order business in Camp Verde. Sedona had a large thriving Gay population and it had been there for decades. But Sally and Amy were big Trump supporters, bragging once, they had five million tax reasons for supporting Trump. They said being a New Yorker, Trump didn't really believe that stuff he was saying about Gays and Lesbians. Ben and Ann didn't know what to say although, late at night in the spring, Ben did swipe their Trump for 2020 and Forever! sign and threw it away in the grocery store's dumpster. The sign was too big to fit in Ben's garbage can.

Ben was too tired, to really greet people and put on what he considered the fake widower act. He delayed the next inevitable get together but promised to see them all soon. He treasured them but just needed some time to settle in with Ann.

So after getting a Moon Dog Pizza delivered, he and Ann called it a night, after going outside to look at the stars. It was a clear but very dark night with little cloud cover. Because of how far away they were from any big city and the lack of ambient lighting, the dark sky exploded with bright stars. Ann and Ben felt they were in a natural planetarium and it was remarkable. Occasionally a satellite or a blinking Jet would pass by on its way to the western coast, but otherwise it was just Ann, Ben and the stars.

Ben was glad that the just two of them had driven out there even though it was originally Don's idea. Ann was glad too, being increasingly concerned over Ben's unwillingness to come out here, since her death, to a place that was so good for his body and soul:

"Ben why did you wait so long to get back out here? Were you afraid?"

"No, I thought it just wouldn't feel the same without you being here. But now, I'm so happy to be here with you."

Ben looked around the driveway for her, but since it was dark anyways, Ann had switched off the virtual reality setting, cause why waste energy when Ben couldn't see her or anybody in this darkness. Why bother? It typically looked like a power outage in the neighborhood because of the lack of street lights. Neighbors had to carry flash lights to avoid falling in the drainage ditches.

All thanks to becoming an officially designated Dark Sky Community where ambient light was minimized (i.e. No street lights) and potential for falling in the dark was maximized.

Then Ann spoke anyways: "Let's go to bed, honey, it's been a long remarkable day." Again, thinking of Don's arrest, Ben's release, Dust Storm, and the long scenic drive to get here.

"Can we stay for a little bit, the Stars are so bright."

And so were just the two of them, shining under the Stars that beamed their approval.

Chapter 23

Getting Acclimated

Ben woke up at 6 am Arizona time (8 am CST), and walked in his under wear to the kitchen to make some instant coffee. He reminded himself to put some ground coffee on the grocery list, so he could start using the French Coffee Press. Kinda of worked like a plunger (Not that kind!) in a small carafe. Luckily, there still was some cinnamon spice instant oatmeal, so he grabbed 2 packets and put it in the microwave.

Just as it beeped, Ann popped in wearing a complete REI hiking outfit including boots. Ben always put on his boots in the garage because otherwise that red rock dust got all over everything.

"Ready for some real physical and spiritual exercise?"

"Yeah, I guess." Ben was not crazy about ending up in Bible study after the walk.

They had made a deal that if Ben went to Bible study after Wednesday morning services, Ann would accompany him, hiking up Cathedral Rock

Trail which was only 10 minutes away on 179. They left early as soon as it turned light, as then, there were likely to be fewer tourists and the sunlight for photos was better.

Ben parked the car after checking for scratch damage from yesterday's sandstorm but the caddy was none too worse for wear. This was another way of saying, the car was already beat up on the outside. Cathedral Rock was one of their favorite walks.

People would come from all over the world and try to feel potential Vortex activity at Cathedral Rock. Ben had seen everything there from energy Gurus to flute playing guides to Yoga instructors teaching classes. It got really crazy and crowded in the spring. So many hikers would get in line that it looked like there was a TSA pre check line on the trail.

Still today in the winter, at this early hour, it was quiet and no matter how many photos Ben took, it never matched the grandeur that his eyes took in on any of the several plateaus. Ben and Ann had hiked not only to the top but all the way around where they would end up by the Oak Creek River, not far from the end of the Verde Valley School Road. Ben walked to the top with Ann and they made their way back down. Ben suggested going on the Ezze-Peeze hiking trail but there just wasn't enough time. Ann didn't want to risk missing her own Kaddish Memorial Prayers at the Temple.

Chapter 24

Temple

The Temple was only a 1 or 2 miles south on 179 from their hike. Ben and Ann had been members for over 10 years. To the extent they had a spiritual home, this was it. It was a small active congregation, even the Unitarian Church that rented space there on Sunday, had almost as many Jewish members as the Synagogue. That was a point of contention. Located across the street from the Episcopal Church, that building looked like it had been shipped there from the Greek Island of Santorini, the Temple was a welcoming place. It had a great Rabbi and her husband Jack acting as a spiritual team. The many volunteers were a particular strength and they had more programs than Temples, 10 times their size. Ann, in particular, was quite popular for her split pea and lentil soups, that she brought for congregational lunches. Before Ann died, Ben would drop her off for Bible study. He would then typically go hiking on either Marge Dawes Trail which made one feel like that they were hiking in a postcard (the Vistas were that good) or Cathedral Rock and pick up Ann when study/services were over..

Ann made herself scarce, while Ben walked into Services so it wouldn't look like he was talking to himself. That was the last thing he needed members talking about. Services had just gotten started. Ben counted and saw that there were 11 people so they did have a minyan (a quorum of at least 10 people necessary to say certain prayers including the Kaddish for Ann. The Kaddish Memorial Prayer, while it is prefaced by announcing who it is being remembered that week, the Prayer itself is a simple one in which worshipers acknowledge the Sanctity of God's Sacred Name). It has been said for at least 1200 years and the name Kaddish is close to the Hebrew word Kadosh meaning Holy. Ben wondered if Ann was listening. He was trying to this time.

After services were over, Ben wanted to quickly leave after talking with Val and Bill. Bill and Val were also from Minnesota and had lived full time in Sedona for over 10 years. Val and Bill loved it there. They had come down to visit and developed an acute case of the all too common Red Rock Fever. They quickly found a beautiful home during the recession and were quite active hiking. They liked being part of the community. Bill acted as a voluntary facilities manager and then some for the Temple while among other things, Val played in the local mandolin orchestra. (The community was lucky to have them) Ann and Val had met years ago, when Ann became friends with Val's mom Esther. Since the 4 of them had all come down there, the 2 couples- Bill and Ben, Val and Ann spent a lot of time together. Now it would be just the 3 of them. Sort of.

But that was it. His soul, such as it was, encouraged him to go. Heck, he had at least stayed for the memorial service. He knew he had promised to stay for the entire Bible Study Class, but enough was enough. His soul was overflowing with thoughts of Ann and Ben didn't want to risk it spilling on the other congregants. He was polite and measured while people came up to him to talk about Ann's death. He knew they meant well but he just wished they could leave him alone. Besides with Ann by him, now- he wasn't really alone.

He felt the need to hike, so he drove to the Marge Dawes Trail for some more steps. Was trying to get 15,000 steps a day. Right up the street from yet another Circle K convenience store, he started the climb, taking the tall steps up about 300 feet. He was glad he had his poles with him. The physical activity especially up the stairs worked his thighs like a stair master. It felt good and helped relieve the tension he felt building from the Religious Service. He felt a little bad about leaving Ann there, but he figured that she could want to stay for Bible study and he just wasn't ready for those types of interactions yet. He thought as a rambling Spirit, Ann could find her own way home. She always had.

But a moment later, she POPPED in. She was back in her REI outfit:

"Hey guy, are you ok? I thought part of the deal was, you would stay for the study session after Services?"

"I know. I just couldn't take any more. I did what I could. I get why, it was important to say the Kaddish Memorial Prayer for you. That was the right thing to do, and I did that but I just couldn't stay any longer. I tried. So I fled like Moses into the wilderness."

Ben theatrically twirled around, bowed and then stared and pointed at the vista in the distance. He could see Chimney Rock and much closer, across the Canyon was the old part of Sedona. It really did look like a picture postcard, it really did.

"Well played Sir, well played!" Ann laughed and then bowed.

"Hey, wanna invite some of the neighbors for a happy hour say around 4pm? I won't be talking to anyone besides you but I can sure listen. I want to catch up on what everyone has been up to."

"Sounds real good to me. I'll set it up when we get back."

Ben knew that the condolence recognition day with their Sedona friends would have to come. Ben sighed. It reminded him that he also still hadn't spoken to their daughter Sue in a long time. Ann and Ben had been estranged for a long time even before Ann's death. Sue had always been the most difficult child. She just couldn't help feeling that she had gotten a worse deal compared to her siblings. Sue had honestly believed that growing up that her parents loved her less. After several high school suspensions, minor drug issues, thefts from her parents, at least Ben was inclined to agree. Some kids are just tougher to raise. Ann remained hopeful until the mess with Chuck.

Even after Sue had moved unannounced to the real Sunshine State Florida, Ben and Ann had made periodic attempts to reconcile (what a funny French word- typically used when a parent gives in to their adult child- usually money.) with Sue. But nothing had stuck. The formal estrangement (another funny French word- the polar opposite of reconcile) when they refused to lend money (think mid five figures) for a SECOND time to her third husband Chuck for a failing real estate venture. Ben did feel guilty when he felt privately vindicated when the venture went belly up. Sue blamed her parents of course when they had turned down the "opportunity of 3rd round of financing.

Ben did call her after Ann's sudden death but she was cold, very cold. So Sue continued to remain an ache on their hearts, one that Ann and Ben mentioned less and less even before her death as time went on.

Anyways, Ben still had his recognition session to contend with. Might as well, be with cheese and crackers.

Chapter 25

Passing Time: Happy hour with the Neighbors

Rather than call, Ben walked over to invite their neighbors after he returned. As a Spirit, Ann could immediately zing herself over, so she stuck around to appreciate the beauty of the Rocks and listen in on some of the conversations. (Hey, there was no cable upstairs.) Anyways, Ben walked over first to invite Mary because when she was working in the garage, (ie grinding, polishing, chiseling and whatever else world famous sculptors do with the music of C. C. R. (A 60's rock group) blaring, she couldn't hear the phone. Mary took off her protective eyewear and stood back, so Ben could admire her latest piece of sculpture work: Mother Earth. Ben more than loved it. It was magnificent. The sculpture had a completely different look when it was turned to the other side. Just as pretty but different. It was like getting 2 sculptures for the price of one.

The flowing lines, the seductive, yet strong onyx piece on one side, reminded him of Ann, on the other himself:

"How much?" Ben had never been able to afford one of Mary's sculptures but this was different. It was Ann in physical form, he wanted it, he needed it, he had to have it. He wanted to have it around because Ann was no longer physically there. His great Aunt Ethel had done the same thing when she commissioned a sculpture of her beloved husband Paul many years before.

"1500 bucks, a special price for you and Ann." Mary liked Ann. Everyone did. This price was a deal. More like a gift really. Her larger pieces typically cost thousands. It barely covered the cost of the Arizona Onyx. Mary was a shrewd business woman, not a charity, so like she said, she wasn't gonna give it away. Ben had once asked Mary how she came up with her prices, Mary, slightly though justifiably miffed, explained that besides the time and materials, the prices reflected her entire life experience. Fair enough. Ben had advised Mary, if she really wanted to mentor young starving artists, she could write a book about the Business of Art. Ben even volunteered to help. Nope, she had said. Why create competition? Again, Mary was a shrewd business woman. So Ben wrote a check, borrowed a 2 wheeler and carted it over to his house. He proudly placed it on the entry table in the living room, underneath a painting an artist claimed to have painted with his toes. Whatever. Anyways, he now had Ann depicted as, Mother Earth with him all the time while he pondered Castle Rock. (Which he and his family called Bob the Rock after a favorite deceased coworker) He hoped Ann would understand why he needed this piece of sculpture. It made him feel more centered especially when Ann wasn't around.

Mary agreed to stop by around 5 o' clock and she was bringing Glenna who was in town photographing native berries for her next vegan cookbook. Ben wondered if she ever fell off the wagon and cooked Beef BBQ. He'd have to ask. Ben bet it would have been great. Anyways, he got ahold of Lisa and Steve who also agreed to mosey over around 5 pm. Steve was getting a little frail, now, but his mind (Outside of Fox) was still in tiptop shape. Don worried a bit about Steve and Lisa, he was fond of them.

Then Ann POPPED in, she noticed the new sculpture right away:

"How much?" Ann was also careful with their money. Rightfully so- Ben was somewhat more of a financial sieve. Left to Ben alone, money just drained away. He thought it was part of the sharing economy. Ann thought that while Ben was generous to a fault, it was a fault and they still had to save something for themselves for the future. When Ben and Ann got married, they agreed that they would join economic forces and each could spend up to $500 without discussing it in advance with the other. They each had had slips i.e. the dining room set (Ann), a computer (Ben, alright a car, too) but it did sometimes irritate Ben that even after 30 years, they had not adjusted the $500 amount for inflation.

"Mary sold it to us for $1500 but there was no tax or transportation cost since she drove it here." Boy that sounded weak. He should have come up with a better argument. At least Ben knew better than to lie on the cost to Ann.

"Her stuff typically sells for thousands." Ben tried next. Claiming the purchase was a financial investment- well, that sounded crass and Ben knew in his heart it was an emotional investment.

"What is it?"

"It's a representation of Mother Earth. I saw it and thought of you."

"Really.." This may have been good or not, Ben wasn't sure.

"Next time, YOU decide to BUY a sculpture of ME, especially over $500, you get my consent, first. Do you understand?" This was not good, but bringing up her unilateral $2000 dining room set would not help. Not at all. He still thought about it, though.

"You know how much I wanted an original by Mary. I tried everything to negotiate a trade but Mary is a formable business woman, in addition to being a great sculptor. I even offered to write her in or out of my next book but no go." Ben was a writer but Mary was not impressed with the offer. At all. "You can't spend words." was Mary's response. So Ben tried again- another tack with Ann:

"I just wanted, needed to physically have you near me. This sculpture does that, it will comfort me when you're not around." Ann had often talked of dying young like her own mother. Those scars never heal. Ben thought for a moment of their daughter Sue but quickly pushed that thought away.

"Ok, just don't do it again." She said firmly yet softer. While still angry, Ann was touched.

"But now, I won't have to." Ben felt he now had Ann both emotionally (Spirit) and physically (Sculpture)- permanently. It wasn't the same, but Ben could make do.

The guests arrived shortly after. Sally and Amy didn't come because they had a previously scheduled Log Cabin Society which was a group of Gay Republicans.

Steve and Lisa were right on time. Ben and Steve had spent many a pleasant afternoon discussing ancient history and Steve was an avid reader, also. Occasionally the 4 of them would have dinner together. At about 515 pm, Mary walked over with Glenna. There too many people for the front porch so they walked around to the back and sat around the table. It was still in the 60's. Ben brought out some cheese and crackers in addition to a bottle of Merlot wine.

"How are you holding up, honey?" Lisa was genuinely concerned about Ben, they all were. Ben nibbled on a piece of cheese and pondered how to answer. He, and nobody else, could see Ann sitting in the corner. Ann looked at him, questioning. Typically in the past, Ann didn't stick round for happy hour, but she was curious to see how everyone was doing and how Ben would react.

"It's been tough but getting better. Besides the overwhelming loss of a loved one, (He didn't like using Ann's name in the past tense when she was sitting right there- it seemed rude in a bizarre way.) there's all the freaking paperwork that goes with it. Closing accounts, turning in papers, proof of death, reviewing our estate plan.. It's a handful and Ann took care of all that. Not to be morbid, but I always assumed I would die first and then Ann would deal with everything. I guess I was wrong…." Ben looked up and only he could see Ann playing an imaginary violin. He shook his head.

Mary took that as a sign that he was upset and patted him on his hand: "There, there Dear… You can let it out. You're not alone. Go ahead and cry. You're among friends."

Ben wasn't about to tell this group or anyone else that he wasn't alone and that Ann was with him. Even in this quirky capital of the world with its highest per capita of healing crystals per resident, this would not go over well.

Steve grabbed some of the Costco cashews that Ben had out: "You know, I was just reading World Archeology Today that they believe they found one of Alexander the Great's campsites in India. They found the remains of a battle elephant, complete with head guard protection."

Thank God for Steve, this unusual nugget gave the group something else to focus on. That was pretty amazing.

Just then Sid came in about a half hour late. He had just finished a photo taking drone flight over a large estate near Enchantment Resort in West Sedona that he was hoping to list as the Realtor. Even a 7% commission split several ways was a lot of money when the house listing price was over $4 million dollars. The group quickly moved to a discussion about how unmanned drones were changing war and real estate.

Then Glenna offered that sales of her wild berry photography series were going pretty well: "Mary and I have been also thinking of making our own gin from wild Juniper berries." Glenna still wasn't used to calling Mary, Mom. There were just too many years she called her Dad or Brad. But Glenna was a good trooper and loved her parent. Kids usually do. They may not always like their parents (sometimes for decades) but they almost always love them.

"You know Glenna, we, I meant- I, used your no bake vegetarian lasagna recipe and it was great. Hard to believe that cottage cheese works as well as ricotta. I'm gonna show off and make it for my law cronies during football season. Should go well with beer. Thanks so much."

"You're welcome." Glenna beamed. She was pleased.

Mary was practical: "You get rid of Ann's clothes yet? And what about all those shoes of hers?"

Ben hadn't done a thing on the clothes: "I'm working on it." It was too painful at first and now, who knows, maybe Ann could come back somehow and need her clothes back? The shoes were a different matter. Ann was a remarkable person with a lot of soul and soles for that matter. She had over 100 pairs of all kinds that she kept on shoe racks in the third bedroom. She had them indexed on the computer by brand and function. That bedroom looked like a miniature shoe shop. Larry's friends had suggested he list them on that used clothing website Poshmark but Ben was wary. In the end, he gave the shoes all to Goodwill right before Ann came back into his life. While he hadn't reclaimed his life, he had at least reclaimed the third bedroom. Ann was not very happy and she told Ben, that like most men, he did not understand how much pleasure and meaning came when a woman put on special shoes.

It was getting colder now, with the setting sun –it wasn't unusual for temps to drop a full 10 degrees by 6pm. Ben wanted to tell them about Ann (he couldn't), wanted to reassure them all that he was doing ok, but he just didn't feel like talking. The party quickly broke up. It was the first happy hour without Ann physically there. She was missed by all. A lot. Ben watched them go home by their bouncing flashlights. It looked like one of those old cartoon sing alongs. It was completely dark now. A nice black blanket covered the neighborhood.

Ben had a bowl of Campbell's vegetarian soup and crackers for dinner. It's funny how old mainstays, from younger days, provide such comfort and relief. Campbell's soup, Jiff peanut butter, Chef Boyardee Ravioli, Tombstone Pizza, Taco Bell and of course, Velveeta, These were the edible reminders of his youth. When times were tough, Ben just felt better eating his comfort foods even when Ann called it, his plastic diet. Eventually Ben and his stomach were going to have to grow up and mature. While Ann teased him of having the stomach of a 12 year old, she understood the importance and reassurance of comfort food. She was good that way. She could be very patient.

Ann was tolerant too in the ways that count. Over the years, Don and Ben had come up with many piss poor schemes to hit the big time. While these ideas usually sprung forth after 2 or 3 beers, one day after a miserable bike ride in the sudden rain, the two boys came up with an idea: the bike umbrella. The two called it their inspiration after precipitation. Even building the prototype out of left over plumbing parts in Don's basement, they excitedly went to Home Depot to purchase the plumbing parts to make 10 more as samples to share with the big retailers: Target, Walmart and the like. But sadly, their research had not included a simple search on Amazon that revealed that bike umbrellas were already being sold for $12.99 each shipping included. Since they had spent $12 per umbrella in plumbing parts, their bike accessory empire was gone before it even got started. And they still had all those plumbing parts. Ann laughed and said if they were serious about making big bucks, they should become plumbers- heck they already had the parts.

Yes, Anne was good in a lot of ways but was not particularly patient when it came to Ben's body when it came to serious health issues. Take his sleep apnea for example. Even after Ben had gained 30 pounds, years ago, she was patient until his snoring could be heard in the neighbor's condo above them. The neighbor sent an angrily letter with just 5 words: STOP NIGHT TIME SNORING. IMMEDIATELY! Ben was not content with causing just Ann to lose her sleep, his snoring was now invading the neighborhood! More ominously, at times, he stopped breathing until he woke up with a snort or Ann yelled to wake him up. When they finally had a serious talk about this, Ben fessed up to occasionally waking up with chest pain sometimes in the middle of the night. Before giving into a sleep study and formal diagnosis, Ben had tried everything. He taped his nose open, he taped his lips shut but he still woke up exhausted. Next he tried the devices he found researching on the internet. Ben started with a wedge pillow but that felt like a domestic version of the Berlin Wall and he didn't like not sleeping next to Ann. Finally, Ben tried what he claimed was a highly rated sleep apnea pillow but in reality was a large air cushion strapped to his back to prevent him from sleeping on it. It looked like a vitamin pill for a dinosaur. Ann made an appointment for a sleep study and sleep specialist the very next day.

They quickly diagnosed sleep apnea and fitted him up with a sleep machine which maintained positive air flow so his airway didn't collapse while he was asleep. Although he looked like an air force pilot lying down in bed with all the tubing, Ann preferred it to the snoring. Now they all slept better including the neighbor upstairs. Ben lost 20 lbs. which also helped.

But when Ann died, he missed her so that he started "forgetting" to use his sleep machine on a regular basis. He figured why bother? When Ann came back the first time, she immediately confronted him on this dangerous practice. Ben like any self-respecting widower denied he was ignoring his health on purpose and immediately started using and occasionally cleaning his sleep machine. Only sometimes. Occasionally, Ben needed a lot of adult supervision.

In any case, tonight Ann POPPED in after he had changed for bed: "Got a big day planned tomorrow?"

"Nothing too special. Breakfast with a cougar, followed by volunteering at V Bar V Ranch. Then I will go out and spread the gravel." It's what Arizonians did instead of cutting the grass.

"Yeah, like Joy would sure appreciate being called a cougar." Joy was 81, certainly not a cougar and was Ann's best friend. Joy, a devout Lutheran was a volunteering machine at the Friends of the Forest, her church and the Resale Shop she ran in Grand Marais, Michigan in the summer. She was a force of nature and she was obligated to give free oatmeal raisin cookies to Ben for the rest of his life, in exchange for legal services, that Ben had previously provided. Joy was turning over the cookie loot at Amigos Restaurant in the old town- Sedona. They were meeting there at 745 am so they could still get the early bird special. Just because Joy had cash, didn't mean she had to give it all away. A bargain was a bargain even at age 81. Joy said bargain hunting was still one of her few not so guilty pleasures available to her. She was gonna grab all the bargains of life she could find in her remaining days. Ben hoped she still had a lot of them left.

"You sure, you can't tell her about us getting back together?" Joy was heartbroken when she found out that Ann died. It wasn't supposed to happen that way. But sometimes it did. Ben was willing to risk the rules, but Ann wasn't:

"Can't risk it. Like I said before it's a clear violation of the Disciplinary Code. Wish I could." Ann was a stickler for following rules:

"The rules are there for a good reason." Ann would often say that even before she died. A person's personality didn't change just because they died. Ann hadn't changed. At her core, Ann was still Ann.

"I understand, just glad you're here."

Ben was tired and clicked off the light, then asked Ann: "Ok if I turn off the lights, now?"

"Little late to the game, aren't we?"

"Never too late to be with you! Good night, honey. Love you. Talk to you tomorrow."

"It's a date."

Ben exhaled and turned on his side. He thought he heard a soft POP but he was already drifting off to sleep. He was asleep in less than a minute.

Chapter 26

V Bar V

It was going to be an interesting day, Ben could feel it with the annual meeting and everything else going on.. So he went for an early short hike while he could. This was before the collect phone call that Ben received from a restricted number. Somehow he had an inkling that Don would be calling him from prison:

"Hey Ben, its Don,,"

"What other good friend would call me collect? How are you doing?"

"OK, I guess, all things considered. It's been 2 months since I got arrested and I'm finally getting used to life in the steel cage." For some reason, Don didn't like admitting he was in prison. He said it made him feel guilty. Don, of course, still thought he had done the right thing by making the "refunds."

"What do they have you doing, there?"

"Oh, they started me in wood shop prison industries but after I got beat up and they heard about my computer programing skills, they put me in the library teaching prisoners how to be a programmer. I'm up to 50 cents an hour which is their highest rate. (There being no minimum wage in prison)."

"Can I get you anything?"

"You could mail me a book on Fortran (An older computer language). The warden wants me to reprogram some of the correctional department mainframes. My attorney is all for it, says it might even help when we get to the sentencing phase of the trial."

"You even got a trial date yet?

"Nah, but he thinks next spring is likely"

"I'll be there."

"Thanks." Then a loud beep. "I gotta get off soon."

"How's Deb?"

"It's been tougher on her, than me. Should have thought about that more before this restorative justice caper. Only thought about the cape. Better go now- bye."

And with that like Batman, he was gone.

Ben was still up early and was at the Amigos (Friends) restaurant by 715 am. He got there early because Ben wanted to visit with Pepe, the owner. Pepe had come to America with his family in his childhood. They had come to America legally and worked hard to climb the American ladder of success. While, his parents after lifetime of hard physical work, were now happily retired in Phoenix, their children were able to climb up the economic ladder further. Pepe's siblings included a cop in Tucson, a teacher in Santa Fe and a nurse in Phoenix who kept a thoughtful eye on their now elderly parents. Pepe had struck out on his own, in his 20's. He had never been one to sit still in school.

As a lark, he had taken a job at the world famous Enchantment Resort outside of Sedona. The hotel put him to work in the kitchen where he found that he loved being a Chef. What he found he didn't love, was having multiple supervisors and ever changing rules.

Pepe desperately wanted to be his own boss and so before he even turned 25, he had opened his own Mexican Café in the old tourist section of Sedona not far from the "Y" fork where Highway 179 connects with Highway 89A. That was 12 years ago, and Pepe had recently signed a 10 year lease extension.

Ben had met Pepe, after emerging from the Hogie Heights Trail one day after a strenuous 8.5 mile hike, he decided to refill his hiking water bladder before undertaking the magnificent 4 mile Dorn Descent into Oak Creek Canyon. Ben ordered his lunch and his burrito had already arrived before he realized he had forgotten his wallet. Pepe was very cool about it, extended credit for 2 hours, and created a patron for life. (Ben driving home for his wallet before going on the 2nd leg of his hike) Now they were fast friends, or at least restaurant friends.

"Buenos Diaz, mi amigo, como esta?" (Good morning my friend, how are you?) Pepe said it slowly for Ben's benefit. While Pepe was bilingual, Ben was not.

"Esta bien." (I am good) How's it going for you?"

| 171

"No complaints. Number of tourists is finally picking up."

"Are they finally done with the alleged traffic calming street repairs in Old Sedona?" In an effort to relieve the pressure of 3 million tourists a year, many of whom liked to drive their cars and try to make left turns, the city had added a number of traffic circles and an alternative driving route.

"Almost, they're done with everything except the plants. The city council is arguing over what qualifies as a native plant that is calming for the road." They both laughed.

"Are you dining alone today? So sorry to hear about your wife passing." Pepe paused, then: "I know it's been a while but how are you really doing?"

"Thanks, I'm hanging in there. (Ben didn't feel like saying he was doing ok today) I've got an old friend meeting me for breakfast."

"You want your coffee and your usual order put in now?"

"I'll take the coffee but I'll wait on ordering the rest of my meal til she comes in." Ben did have to admit there was something really satisfying about being able to order the "usual" and the restaurant staff knowing what he wanted. It was like they were saying a person mattered and they took the time to remember a person's favorite meal. It was comforting and reassuring.

Shortly after a waitress brought Ben his coffee, Joy walked in, carrying his treats. It was banana bread. It was 730 am, right on time. Ben liked that. Sometimes, he swore the only 3 people who were on time for appointments in the entire world were himself, Joy, and Ann. Showing up on time was a sign of respect and consideration for other people. It told them, that one respected their time, too. Ann had a group of friends who ran late. Always late, sometimes up to 1 or 2 hours. One of them, once had the gall to tell them, that they would have been almost been on time but they HAD to stop at a garage sale. Seriously. But now, Ann wasn't going to be consistently on time anymore. She explained that like a lot of things in her life after death, it wasn't always in her control. There were mandatory meetings, energy failures, traffic jams etc. Ben believed her, of course, but it was tough, real tough. Although they tried to make plans, Ben never knew when exactly Ann could POP in. So they used a range of time, usually like see you in the morning or talk to you tonight. Still, it was much better than nothing. Much better. Ben wasn't complaining. He didn't think he ever would-even if this was all he got. Ben was getting much better at appreciation, really gratitude.

But this morning, there was an empty chair where Ann would have sat. Sometimes it was still hard, even after Ben started seeing Ann again. Ben stood up to give Joy a hug. She felt lighter and more fragile. This was worrisome.

"Hey Joy, good to see you. Thanks for the invite. Feels different, huh."

Joy's eyes dampened: "I'm glad you could finally make it down here."

Ben didn't make any excuses: "It was just too tough…I love our place and it's good to see you but it just doesn't feel right it being just the 2 of us.." Truthfully, Ben was surprised that Ann wasn't listening in a corner like last night.

"I still can't believe she's gone…" Joy's eyes misted again. "I remember the first time we saw your home, the 3 of us sitting in the living room, staring at Castle Rock. We were all mesmerized by the beauty. A lot of good times, we shared there.." Joy was the person who got Ann and Ben's oldest daughter first to travel down there. They were enchanted and when Ben came down, he was, too.

"So what gives, the deal was you owed me oatmeal raisin cookies not banana bread?"

"Well, the bananas were about to go bad, and to be honest, it hurts my back to make the individual cookies, these days." Joy had never been a complainer but just simply modified her daily life as she aged.

"Joy, I'm sorry, I didn't know. So I believe you are still in compliance with our deal." Ben hoped she hadn't put in any nuts in the bread. "Look Joy, even without Ann being here, we will still get together and we will still be good friends. I promise." Ben thought he was being sincere and he probably was. But while Ben genuinely was very fond of Joy and shared many common views, the fact remained that Ben and Joy didn't have the same history that Joy shared with Ann. It just wasn't the same.

Then they chatted about their kids while they ate their meals and at 8:30 am, Joy got up to go to her regular workout at Curves work out studio. While she could no longer hike the way she did 10 years ago, she did try to exercise and walk every day. Joy sometimes said if you want to be vital, you had to take care of your vitals. True enough.

Ben paid his bill said goodbye to Pepe and jumped in his car for the half hour drive to V Bar V Ranch. Ann POPPED in for the ride just as he left the parking lot:

"Where were you? I thought for sure, you would show up to see how your friend was doing."

"I really, really wanted to but I didn't trust myself. I was afraid you or I would blurt something out and I can't let that happen. After you and the kids, I care more about Joy than anyone. How's she doing?"

"She's doing. It's been tough. She misses her best friend and we both know nothing can replace you. In addition, her body is breaking down for good and she hates that. You know that Joy has always been fiercely independent. Her backaches won't even let her make cookies anymore."

"Oh, the poor dear. Although I don't like to use them-maybe I can implant some pleasant memories of the two of us to cheer her up."

"I didn't think you like to do that."

"I don't. Maybe, I'll do a fly by, and check and see how she's doing."

"Hey, it's your best friend."

"I'll catch up with you later. I don't like hanging at V Bar V anyways. It gives me the creeps." Ann wasn't kidding. She said she felt a strange disturbance there but wouldn't explain it any further. So today she POPPED and she was gone.

Driving down on Highway 179 East, since he had time, Ben decided to stop at Yavapai Vista for a quick look. Yavapai Vista was on the other side of the road from the more famous Bell Rock Trail. It was a short 5 minute hike, rather a stroll, to the first plateau where he could see many of the famous Buttes. He had taken hundreds of photos in the past and likely would be taking thousands more. But not today. He gazed at Bell Rock, Bunny Ears and Courthouse Butte. He breathed in, he breathed out then he had some deep thoughts. Ben still didn't know what they were.

Then he turned his attention to the left and looked at the majestic Buttes further away. There were many Trails that intersect here including Slim Shady, Baldwin Trail and the Yavapai Vista Trail if one went further. He took a deep breath and looked at his watch. It was getting close to 9 am. He better leave if he wanted to be on time to V Bar V Ranch.

Highway 179 was not too crowded so he made good time. He passed through the Village of Oak Creek, the Hilton, and the Beaver Flats shortcut to Cottonwood. Still on 179 until the juncture with I-17, he went straight, underneath the I-17 highway and soon he was on a 25 mph gravel road. He passed the usually uncrowded Bell trail, and the road that took visitors to Montezuma's Well. The Caddy bounced over 2 one lane bridges over the Beaver Creek, that looked like they were built from a rusty Erector Set and then you were there at V Bar V. Almost. There was a big cattle gate that had to be unlocked and then only ½ mile down a worse gravel road and visitors were already there.

V Bar V was Ben's favorite archeological site in the world. He had been volunteering there as a Guide for 5 years. V Bar V had been a working ranch for almost a 100 years and that probably helped to protect the over 1000 petroglyphs that were in plain view, on the side of a large rock formation, so close to the Beaver Creek.

The Petroglyphs (Carved as opposed to Pictographs which are painted) were all in the unique Beaver Creek Style which meant, most of the animals were in pairs, their arms stretched up and there were lines from one set of animals to another. To the far right, there was a large geometric pattern with figures around it, and nearby archaic scratches that go back thousands of years. To the far left on the side there appears to be a woman in traditional Hopi styling and a line that may connect it to a baby. Otherwise, there were no humans represented. The figures were carved from 800 to 1400 AD.

There are several factors that made this site unique:

The first was the sheer number of animals and how they were paired. The Hopi tribe traced their ancestry to some of their clans including the Bear, Turtle and Snake.

The second is the fact that the site was apparently holy, in that the ground was softer near the figures, which served as archeological evidence that only the favored few Religious Shamans could approach the petroglyphs.

Third, there appeared to be a real fear that Spirits of the Underground would come up so all of the rock cracks had been filled with other rocks. Moreover, the Native Tribe did not live by their Holy site as was typically the case but rather over a mile away.

Fourth, and most importantly, there was an astronomical clock that assisted the Anastasi Tribe as to when to plant their crops in the formerly irrigated fields that were nearby and had been in use for hundreds of years.. A part of the rock clock had sadly fallen off recently due to heavy rains, after being in place for approximately 800 years.

Ben loved to come early, sit on a stump and study the petroglyphs. On rare occasions usually when he was almost asleep, Ben thought the figures spoke to him. Mostly not. As noted, the petroglyphs were done in the unique Beaver Creek style. Animals were done in pairs with their upper arms stretched upwards as if they were asking for something. (Prayer?) There were snakes, turtles, deer, even tall birds with rays coming out of their heads. Other times, he would just listen to the creek gurgle and occasionally, he would just nap. Tourists usually started coming at 10:30 am but and Ben would tell them as much or as little as they wanted to know. Wise visitors might just listen and feel the site. Ben was just as happy as when no one showed up. It was a peaceful and meaningful place.

At 1 o' clock, the next guide arrived. Many of them were far more knowledgeable than Ben about the Tribe, what was known about their culture, the petroglyphs and how the calendar worked.

After his shift was completed and he turned over his keys and walkie talkie, Ben took his car down the bumpy road back to 179 and then on to his house. He popped a Tombstone pizza in the oven, drank a Kilt Lifter beer and got ready to rake the yard as he had planned. Ben had not understood how much maintenance- their no maintenance yard took and if it wasn't for the help of Jose, the gardener, the place would have been a festering place of weeds, leaves and branches.

Ben started by getting the garbage can and placing it in the middle of the yard. He next grabbed the larger branches and using his inner Michael Jordan, tossed them from a distance into the can. After finishing the branches, it was on to raking the leaves, pinecones, and peapods that were everywhere in both the front and back yard. Being in the Verde Valley, didn't mean no trees or weeds. Next, it was onto picking the weeds. Here, he had a little help.

Thanks to Lisa, his neighbor, he had purchased a weed picker that would pull out weeds by the roots if you aimed it just right. It was a deceptively simple tool comprised of a long piece of wood with a short metal V shaped prong at the end. It worked deceptively well. Sometimes simple works best. This method combined with a trash grabber, avoided Ben having to bend down every 10 seconds to dig into the gravel with his fingers or a hand tool. Instead of calling it his God send, Ben called the two tools his back send. This effort still took close to an hour.

Then, it was on to his favorite part of the cleanup, raking the gravel. After a short water break, he grabbed the garden rake and got started. It was mindless yet mindful work. While he pulled the rake, he trolled his thoughts. Ben just let his mind drift. Raking really didn't take much skill. Sometimes when he raked gravel, he thought of particular issues, he was dealing with. But today, was a thought drifting day and he just let his mind go. It was good to be back, it would have been better if Ann was fully here, but it was still good enough.

There remained the trimming of the shrubs. This had formerly been in the Ann department, and not only was she good at it, she seemed to enjoy it, too. For Ben though, it came down to this basic fact: he sucked at trimming and the more he tried, the worse he got. He just plain hated it. He was not one of those people who believed sufficient yard work would make one a better person. Maybe he could ask Jose to come over soon and just trim the shrubs. That sounded like an acceptable plan. Anything was better than Ben doing it.

After 3 hours of moderate yard work, Ben decided he would take a hot shower before dinner. Actually, he wanted to take a bath and sip a scotch as he read a spy novel while soaking but as Ann had noted many times, sitting in your own dirty water, isn't going to get you clean. So given the amount of sweat and dirt he was carrying, Ben decided a shower would be quicker and cleaner. He had usually too quick showers in contrast to his long baths. More ecologically sound. This time though, he decided to shave while in the shower. Ben used Barbasol Shaving Cream which was the same brand his father used. Just smelling it, gave him pleasant memories of watching his father shave years ago. Still, he was surprised he wasn't ready for dinner, until 6:30 pm and it was already dark again.

Just then his cell rang. It was a 305 Miami area code, was it Sue his daughter? Couldn't be but it was:

"Hi Dad, its me. (Even after not speaking for months, Sue expected him to recognize her voice.)"

"Well this is a pleasant surprise, how are you?"(Only a small serving of guilt) He settled down in one of the outdoor chairs for what he hoped would be a long call.

"We're fine though we lost the house." (She too could serve guilt. Somehow this was Ann and Ben's fault that Sue and her husband had placed a second mortgage on their house for a "sure thing "investment. One thing for sure was Ben and Sue were never going to see the $30,000 they previously "lent" them.

Sue continued:

"We're both working again and he has finally given up his dream to be yet another mega Florida real estate Developer. I'm working at the library with great benefits and Chuck is at Home Depot in sales. But enough about us, what about you? I've heard a rumor that you believe that you and Mom are back together, is that true?" (There it was- that screechy voice of disbelief. Ben knew it well, actually too well.)

"Well, we can't explain it but yes it's happened and we're happy, very happy."

"Dad..(The Whiney voice. Ben hated that whiney voice. This voice was different than the disbelieving voice but just as annoying. He had heard it a lot when she was in High School.)

"We don't need anyone's permission." Ben said in a huff

"Permission? Come on Dad, You don't call for months about how we are doing and what do you bring up first- not needing permission? We're not back in High School! You can't control us anymore either." And with that she hung up. Being cut off was probably the most enjoyable part of the call, Ben thought. When you got right down to it, Sue could be a bitter pill that he and Ann had to swallow every now and then. It just didn't always taste so good even though they knew they loved her and that she was a good person

Then even though it was late, he decided to cook some hotdogs on the grill. He decided to take out his aggression on some decayed animal flesh. That daughter of theirs! Hopefully a charcoal meal would settle him down. It is usually did. Turning his attention to dinner, He was surprised when the grocery store in the Village started carrying Hebrew National Beef Hot Dogs. They were kosher, sort of, and although they wouldn't pass muster with his religious daughter, they, too were a fond memory of his youth, even if they were full of nitrates. Ben wondered if the ancient pharaohs ate hot dogs and whether those nitrates helped to preserve the mummies. Worth a thought. Ben fired up the grill and started ripping open a bag of Kale salad.

He was trying to do better with his daily diet. He needed to. It was a constant struggle trying to avoid the carb and sugar laden foods, he loved best. To be honest, Ben also knew his daily salt intake was also way out of whack, But he no longer had Ann to keep him calorically honest. It was a thankless job but she did it well. Someone had to. Speaking of which:

"I'm semi impressed with your food choices tonight except for the main course. How many more nitrates will you need to preserve your body for eternity?" Ann was lounging in one of the microfiber chairs.

"Funny, I've been volunteering and doing yard work all day. Any chance you could zap the top and sides of those shrubs?"

"Sorry, no can do…. That's bargaining unit work for earthlings only. Spirits can only advise. Besides, this is the closest you'll ever get to trimming Nature's natural hair."

"Very funny. What did you find out about Joy?"

"She's hanging in there but it's been a tough year for her physically and my death didn't help."

"Anything, you can do?"

I'm still kicking around the idea of some memory implants."

"You did say memory implants?"

"Oh, stop it. Is it that the only gland you think about?"

"It could be... why don't you ever give me some of those memory implants?"

"All kidding aside, the problem is, some people get too dependent on them and suffer from withdrawal when they're removed or not freshened up. Nothing lasts forever."

"Hey, guess who I heard from?"

"I have no idea"

"It was Sue, remember her? Our daughter, I was really surprised."

"Why did she call?" The ache was still there. Then Ann answered her own question:

"I bet Larry her brother put her up to it."

"I'm sure you're right. They were always close, even when they weren't plotting against us. That sly dog." Ann was much faster on tuning in on the family dynamics.

"What did she say?"

"She wanted to talk about us. She's concerned about us."

"Yep, must been Larry. He always was the calculating one. What did you tell her?"

"Just what I told the others. I don't know how it happened but it did and we're happy- end of story. I told her we didn't need anyone's permission. She took exception to that and hung up. Sorry if I miffed it."

"How she's doing?"

"Pretty good, considering. They lost the house and declared bankruptcy. They're renting a mobile home. She's working as a library aid with benefits and he is a salesman at Home Depot. She really sounded ok before losing her temper and hanging up."

"That's good. At least she knows. Hope I get to talk to her next time. Let me know before you call, I can try and listen in." A mother's heart is always open...

"Hey, I was thinking about us… Wanna go on a date tomorrow?"

"What are you thinking?"

"Well, I was thinking a nice drive to Jerome in the morning with lunch there."

"Ha. You just want to see your favorite Nellie Bly again."

"Come on, it's a beautiful drive and I haven't seen her Kaleidoscope store in over 2 years. I need a more colorful world. I'll let you choose lunch."

"As you know full well, I don't eat lunch."

"You could enjoy watching me eat."

"That sounds appetizing."

"Well, you could at least look at the views…"

"That's enticing…"

"Pleeeese."

"Oh, all right. But I'll have to get some more energy tonight and you better go to sleep now. I want you well rested and alert when you drive up that hill. You gotta promise not to give anyone the finger this time."

"Alright, I'll try not to- but no guarantees…Sometimes those drivers provoke me. Thanks much. See you in the morning."

Ben went into the bathroom, brushed his teeth and then slowly crawled into bed.

Ann snapped her fingers and turned off the lights.

Ben's last thought before falling asleep, was how could she do that?

CHAPTER 27

JEROME

Ben had always loved the magic of kaleidoscopes so he had always loved Nellie Bly. It was simply put, the finest and largest kaleidoscope store in the world. They had kaleidoscopes ranging in price from $10 to $10,000 that pieced the world together in different colors and angles. They even had kaleidoscopes that you assembled yourself out of candy! When Ben looked through any of these contraptions, he felt he was an eager eight year old boy again.

Any ways, Nellie Bly was located in Jerome. The City of Jerome was an old, wild, gold/ copper/silver mining town and it lived precariously on the edge of the steep Cleopatra Hill. Native Americans had long found the pretty rocks there worth trading for- first followed by the Spanish who were always looking for real gold. Mining activity started in 1876 and by 1920 over 15,000 people lived there. But then, especially after World War 2, the gold/silver/copper mines shut down. By the early 50's, population was down to less than a hundred. But the loyal residents never gave up in trying to maintain their city and retain its old buildings. After an effort to make it as a "Ghost town", counter culture artists moved there in the late 60's, attracted by the low costs and majestic views from the Red Rocks of Sedona to the distant San Francisco Mountain Peaks. When hippies discovered capitalism, watch out for your wallets! The bustling destination (at least on weekends) now had 500 residents and there were many art galleries and restaurants' galore. But it was a perilous drive to get there on the old 89A. Ben loved it. It was about an hour from their house and roughly 100 years of history to really get to Jerome.

Ann was waiting for Ben in the car. She was wearing an attractive blue and white head scarf.

"Thanks, honey, this will be fun. What's the headgear for?"

"I'll have you know it's a genuine French Silk Virtual Scarf lent to me by my good French friend Paulette."

"Ok…It looks nice on you." Fumbled recovery.

And they were off (especially Ben). They were driving first on Highway 179 going west still on one of the most scenic drives in America. (At least, that is what the travel magazine wrote) The Red Rocks, the sky, the curves of the road, Ben assumed his pleasure endorphins were being released at a heavy, steady rate. Later they would switch to 89A. Driving there with his beautiful dead, life partner, Ben was at peace with himself and the world.

"So Ben, are you going keep the house?" So just then reality (sort of) had to creep in. But it was a fair question.

"Truthfully, I hadn't given it, a lot of thought. I sure enjoy being there with you around."

"Well, maybe you should sell...It's a fairly large amount of money to be spending on keeping it up, if you're not going to use it on a regular basis." As usual Ann was right. Tough but accurate.

"I suppose, I could rent it out more but with the wear and tear-I just hate that.."

"Look at the numbers. It's about $12,000 each year to carry it and with me dead, we no longer receive my social security of $3000 per month. In addition, you'll only be receiving a survivor's portion of my pension (only 75%). And your arbitration income has been less than you thought..."

Ouch.

"That's true but jeez, can't we just enjoy the day and the drive? I promise, I will give it some serious thought."

"Ok, but you can't keep on pretending that things are not going to change."

They were at the famous "Y" turning circle where 179 ended, where a driver could circle around to the left to newer West Sedona and then on to Cottonwood and beyond, or circle to the right through old Sedona and then up the Oak Creek Canyon and then along the mountain to Flagstaff (Also a magnificent drive).

Their plan was to drive to Cottonwood, so first they had to endure several miles of restaurants, gift shops, grocery stores, hotels on the way until they again hit open country. Hidden here were ranches, a state park and fish hatchery and one of finest birding areas of North America where almost 200 kinds of birds traveled on their way to distant locales. Somewhere warmer Ben hoped.

Before they knew it, they were in actual Cottonwood, where they continued on old 89A. They took a left at Walgreen's and they drove though the industrial part of Cottonwood such as it was and finally started up the famed Cleopatra's Hill. This was Benny's favorite part of drive. It was exhilarating but also frightening with the zigs and zags sometimes only having inches to spare from a fall that could be hundreds of feet. Locals behind him were in a hurry and honked but he ignored them. If Ben didn't tell others how to live their lives, they had no right in attempting to honk him into losing his. Showing a new found maturity, Ben only gave one driver the finger. It was hard to believe prior to Highway I-17 being built, that 89A was the only way to get from Flagstaff to Jerome and then (for a while) the state capitol of Prescott. It added hours and white fisted driving to make the trek under the former route.

The streets and sidewalks of Jerome were so narrow that it was nearly impossible to pass anyone going in the opposite direction. Travel Expert Rick Steves would recognize Jerome as a sister city to those Italian Terraced Hill Side Cities, he was always yapping about. But the Vistas were that spectacular. Both Ann and Ben could see forever.

Many of the buildings had been or were in the process of being preserved. Ben thought the City Residents and Jerome Historical Society should be officially commended for their efforts and wisdom in saving so many buildings.

Then it was time for Nellie Bly. Ann gave Benny 45 minutes to observe, test drive and maybe buy a kaleidoscope. She was going to hang out in some nearby clouds, enjoying the view, and would catch up with him at Stem Wine Bar and Restaurant. Ben would have preferred the Haunted Hamburger for lunch which had a better view and a better hamburger, but a deal's a deal. Whatever- maybe he could grab a Pabst beer at Ben and Jerry's which claimed to be the oldest family owned bar in Arizona, tracing its roots to 1939. The Oldest overall bar in Arizona was in nearby Prescott which had the Palace which was founded in 1864. Located in the middle of Whiskey Row, it had been painstakingly restored.

Ben went inside Nellie Bly and was immediately enchanted. As always. He tried every kaleidoscope on display whether he could afford it or not. He had purchased many over the years, both for himself and for gifts. He still had nothing to compare to the Kaleidoscope Howitzer that his sister had mounted in her backyard. Ben was jealous of his older sister's possession as only a little brother could be. Maybe someday… He was gonna first have to wait a while until Mother Earth, his wife, accepted Mother Earth, the sculpture. Though he found an interesting oak wood one for $175, he knew he had better wait. Maybe after, one of his novels sold…

Ben walked up the street and walked into Stem and asked for a table for two in their small outside dining area. It was a fine bistro but just wasn't his style. Stem had nice red tablecloths, dried flowers and fake grapes. To Ben, this said it all.

It was however Ann's choice, and when she POPPED in there- she was pleased, immensely. Ben had left his menu out on the page with the daily specials so Ann could see it and pulled his phone out after he ordered so he wouldn't look strange speaking to an empty chair. He had used the ruse before.

"So, did you acquire anything special?" Still wearing her French headscarf, Ann peered through her virtual sunglasses. Although no one else could see her, Ben had to admit she looked very chic in it.

"Just you! No, not today. I've been spending all money on my new French girlfriend, they're very expensive."

Ben put the phone down as the waiter came to serve their meal. Although Ann was not eating, she had ordered the meal. It looked like smoked trout on top of some weeds. It tasted, however, pretty dang good. He would have preferred the deep dish pizza, the 2 women were having at the other table. (They do have great pizza) He took his phone out again when the waiter left.

"Well, maybe you should start looking for a newer, less expensive girl friend."

"I am fine with the one, I've got."

"I'm serious."

"Well then, I am too. Look, we've discussed this before….I don't want to…I don't need to…I'm not ready."

"Ok, when will you be ready? As I told you long ago before I died, that if something happened to me, I would want you to be with someone."

"I AM with someone."

"Yeah right. It's not the same and you know it. Besides there could be some incredible fringe benefits."

"It hasn't even been that long since the required year long mourning period."

"That's rich- my husband going pulling out the religion card, when all I want, as his dead wife, is for him to TRY and go out with someone."

"Look, I AM JUST NOT READY."(A bit louder than Ben intended but that dead wife of his was so stubborn.)

Patrons turned to stare.

"Besides more importantly, remember how you wouldn't do anything to risk our relationship?....Well, I won't either. "

"You won't be changing anything, I promise. You won't be risking our relationship. Our love is written in stone."

"But stone crumbles."

"Exactly." (What her point was, Ben wasn't sure but he could still be irritated anyways.)

They didn't talk the rest of the meal.

Ben went for a walk to clear his head but claimed he was just taking some more pictures. Photo taking was usually a good excuse for walking out of almost anything. The Vistas were that good.

Then he received a call from that special and expensive restricted prison number (Remember it was collect). Don did not waste any time on idle chit chat:

"What kind of guy has his dead wife spy on his best friend?"

"And a big hello to you, too. What are you talking about?"

"I know she's been here. I sensed her presence like a tingle on the back of my neck. I couldn't see her or hear her, but she's been here hasn't she?"

"We've been worried about you. We just wanted to make sure you are safe, especially after you got jumped in woodshop."

"Who's we?"

"Come on, you know its Ann. She cares about you."

Don was partially mollified, after all, they were doing it for his own good.

"Well, OK, just give me a heads up in advance when you or Ann are doing this."

"Hey, I saw your face on Good Morning America TV show. Pretty impressive segment- Robin Hood angle and all that." Somehow the news organizations had heard about what Don had done. He was a celebrity after his 3 minutes of televised stardom. Don had fought the big bank on behalf of the little guy. Don wasn't a crook, he was a minor folk hero.

"I do have a pretty face. Gotta go, I'm saving my telephone time for Deb."

Ben started to ask how Deb was but he was already gone.

Ben and Ann finally talked some more, when it was just the two of them in the car:

"Look Ben, I'm not messing with you. I'm only doing this because I love you. I simply don't like seeing you being on your own."

"Don't you think, I know that? That's why it bugs me. I am not alone. I just do not want to risk losing you, losing us."

He started backing up the car and then started moving slowly forward. No one was gonna to rush him, not other drivers or Ann either.

Still he started to mellow as he saw the Red Rocks again. If his dead wife wanted to get him a girlfriend, that wasn't the worst thing in life. Actually, pretty thoughtful on her part. He just wasn't ready yet.

Chapter 28

The Routine

By the time they took the scenic byway of 179 and passed several Vortexes, They were both in a better mood by the time they got home. Was it related? Might be. Hard to say, but neither of them was going to turn away a good mood. Ann in particular, saw that it was a great opportunity to renegotiate the house duties:

"Ben, will you do me a favor, and get a pen and paper?"

Ben acutely sensed, a "list" discussion coming.

"Sure Honey. What for?" What the heck, he was still in a good mood.

"I was thinking we could make a list of what needed to be done around here. We haven't been here since before I was dead. It's a wonderful home, we need to take care of it. This list will help."

Fair enough, Ben thought but it had the dreaded "list" word that like many husbands, he had always feared. With good reason. Still, maybe if he went along, she'd be willing to put on a virtual Tango show tonight. Ann was a great dancer. Ben, sadly, was not. But he liked to watch.

"Sounds like a great idea." She couldn't believe he really wanted that. Ben got a small scratch pad that he hoped, would limit the number of duties.

"OK, let's get started. Shouldn't be more than 12." He didn't fall for it, but she didn't care how many pages it took on the notepad, the work still needed to get done. Ben conceptually knew that but emotionally just wasn't into it. Anne took the lead:

"1 Dishes- you load and unload. I'll supervise.

2 Meal prep/cooking. While it's solely for your benefit, to the extent I'm around, I'll supervise.

3 Shopping. I'll help you make the list and help you pick out the fruits and vegetables. I've noticed you've been having far too many frozen meals and pizza. Way too many Carbs. It's also surprising how much salt lurks in frozen foods. I know you've been trying but you can do better.

4 Laundry. Since I'm a Spirit- you're on your own for this one. Don't forget to hang your shirts up right away after coming out of the dryer. Your skin isn't the only thing that's been wrinkled lately. I'll make time to supervise you making the bed. Your sheets have been sagging, lately.

5 Garbage/ car maintenance. Just keep up your good work and keep that Caddy going..

6 Bill paying. Sorry but I can't do it since I've been legally declared dead. I can help by supervising you. Say, I have noticed, you've been using different credit cards to pay. Please try to stick with the Costco card, it gives us the most points.

7 Taxes. I'm still dead so I can't pay. Any problems see our son in law David, he's the CPA of the family.

8 Yard work. I still don't like ladders and you can handle most of it. To the extent you can't, get Jose the neighborhood gardener.

9 House work. You know, I had a bad back before but now I don't even have one. You're going to have to vacuum /clean the floors, tidy up and then this new activity called dusting. The current once a month doesn't cut it.

That's all I can think of for the moment. Huh, that's only 9 items. Got anything else, you want to add to the list?"

"I'm not sure, let me think, and get back to you."

Ann squinted. Was he messing with her? She couldn't tell if Ben was being serious or just pulling her leg, as it were. The problem was, Ben wasn't sure if he was serious or not either. He had always hated lists, even as a child (maybe he too, suffered from highly spirited child syndrome) but he knew that the work needed to get done. Why couldn't they just deal with the work organically and wait for it to get done, itself?

The problem was, while he may have gotten away with that as a young married couple, in passively dumping everything, he didn't like, on Ann, that wasn't fair. He had tried to improve his share in recent years. Still it also wasn't going to work that way now either. He just had to get his act together and get the work done or hire it out with less income coming in now.

Still with a list, there was a plan and that was better for everyone. They took the rest of the of the day off

Ben ordered Chinese and they watched Netflix until the wee hours. It felt good. Just like old times.

They weren't in bed til 2 am.

Chapter 29

Another Nightly Routine

At 3 am, Ben woke up to pee as usual. He thought it was strange that it was his bladder that reminded him of his mortality. When he was younger, he could sleep all night without waking up to pee. Now that he was older and his plumbing was wearing out, he had to wake up at least once a night, sometimes more to pee. His bladder and prostate were daily acknowledgments to Ben that like his body parts he was mortal and that someday he would be returned to the earth. Wasn't sure how he felt about that. He also wasn't sure what happened when he died. Worrying about it wasn't going to change anything. You still came out of this life one way. Still he couldn't help wondering if the older male plumbing issues were somehow just basic design flaws. He'd have to talk it over with Ann. As a Spirit who had died she might have some further interesting thoughts as to what is mortality. Something to think about but not hopefully at 307 am.

Chapter 30

Friends of the Forest

That morning both Ann and Ben managed to wake up at 8 am. He loved sleeping in late with Ann. Since her return, he was sleeping so much better. Two could sleep better than one. Ben no longer took sleep for granted. It was important as proper nutrition. When Ben now didn't get enough sleep now, it took longer to get it back. As usual Ann was dressed first but even Ann conceded it was quicker to put on a virtual outfit than actual clothes. After morning coffee, they talked about the Friends of the Forest Annual Meeting that was coming up later that day. It was a picnic. These were some talented folks who put in tens of thousands of hours each year. Although Ann and Ben had been volunteering for 5 years, there were many active seniors in their 70's and 80's who were in their 20th year or more of volunteering. The volunteers manned the information desk, gift shops, tested water, took photos, repaired nets, counted species (including tourists), picked up trash, identified and acted as guides at archeology sites such as Honanki and V Bar V and just generally made themselves useful.

But one group in particular did remarkable work that was solely needed, and that was the Graffiti Patrol. While people came from all over to admire the Rocks, the hiking and biking trails and Archeology sites, there were some whose desire for immortality extended to vandalism. (Graffiti) Surprisingly, Graffiti in the area goes as far back as Spanish explorers in the 16th Century. That doesn't make it right and left unchecked, Graffiti would mar the nature seeking experience.

That's where the Graffiti Patrol came in, by volunteers painting and repairing sites, quickly and quietly often in tough to get to areas. These members received specialized training in how to remove and cover paint. Although Ben tried, he had a hard time keeping up with these nimble Billy goats that were up 20 years older and certainly far more skilled.

Many of these volunteers had active and impressive work careers, prior to settling in Sedona. Ann and Ben were reminded of this fact when they went that day to the annual meeting held at Forestry housing located by V Bar V. People had been community leaders and company executives. There were Police Officers and Nurses, Retired Professors and Factory Workers, CEOs, Artists all drawn to a place and community where they could still contribute their passion and time.

After hearing the usual reports and plans for next year, it was time to eat under big white tents. Then they handed free swag to those with lucky lottery numbers and more importantly, fed the volunteers. There was chicken, hamburgers both veggie and meat, hotdogs and 3 kinds of lasagna (meat, vegetarian and this being Sedona-vegan)

Ben went through the line, and not knowing anyone, asked if he could join a table. The other people there were all very friendly, active, accomplished retirees but 3 things stuck out:
1. Many of the most active had been there less than 3 years.
2. A majority of the volunteers were unencumbered by children.

3. Most were nature enthusiasts into hiking, biking, golf, photography, geology or into the arts.

As the table started discussing playing couples' golf and bridge, Ben picked up his phone so he could talk to Ann who was sitting unseen in the empty chair:

"Maybe you should take up golf or bridge?"

"I'd rather watch paint dry."

"Oh, come on, they seem like nice people.. Why don't you invite them over for happy hour?'

"I'm happy enough the way it is.."

"Cheer up Mr. Grumpy. Tell you what, let's go home and we can tangle with some tango. I might even put on one of my racy new virtual outfits."

Ben tried to look serious: "Yes, that sounds like a proper plan. I can be home in less than ½ an hour."

He looked at the friendly faces and made his apologies: "I'm sorry, I've got a client who needs my immediate attention." Ben stood up to go.

Gary, a wireless engineer started walking with him to his car: "You do realize that's there no cell service here, right? Busted!" With that Gary punched him in the shoulder and left.

Back at the table, Gary's wife asked him what they talked about.

"You know, guy stuff." That could cover a variety of topics from Porsches to Prostates.

"Honey, Ben is the sad man who lost wife his over a year ago. Some people say he thought he was talking to her after she died. Poor soul"

Gary wondered to himself, to whom, Ben had been talking. He had the wisdom to say nothing.

Ben sped but still did not beat the tango dancer home.

When he walked into the house, all the shades had been drawn, the room was dark, and a lit disco ball was spinning near the top of their 25 foot vaulted ceiling. Colors danced across the walls. Then, the room erupted into Tango music and Ann was now in a shimmering, reflective, tight silver metallic dress that ended above the knee. It was simply awesome. There was a large feather of some sort and she was stomping her stilettoes, to the extent she could. It was kind of tough to do on carpeting.

"Hola!! Senor, do you wish to see the Tango?" Ann gave asly, seductive smile, then:

"Do you wish to feel the Tango?"

This was beyond awesome, it was perfecto!

"You betcha!" he cried, letting a little Minnesotan slip in.

Ann coiled her lithe, virtual body like a spring around him: "Does Senor wish to danza (dance), the Tango?"

| 203

Ben still in the tiled entry way, stomped his hiking boots in affirmation:

"But of course, I do. Just give me a minute and I'll have these boots off in a Jiffy!" Who says jiffy any more? Another Minnesota slip.

"I thought Jiff was Americano Peanut butter."

"Well, I am nuts for you…"

While Ann had a dancer's soul and could dance exceedingly well, virtual or not, Ben couldn't. This was, too bad, for Tango is very intoxicating. It is also exceedingly, technical. This is where Ben had his biggest problems, he was always 2 steps behind and was trying too hard. The spinning, the stopping, the stomping was too much. Finally, he simply said: "No mas! (No more)" and collapsed on the couch.

"Ann, will you tango just one more dance for me, please, something slow?"

"Sure, I call this: Last Tango in Sedona…" Ann, somehow, got the music changed to the opening theme of the real Last Tango in Paris and she started dancing, slowly at first.

Later, this is what Ben would most fondly remember. Ann dancing in that nice taut, virtual metallic dress and rubbing her hands slowly along her body while she danced the Tango slowly. Slyly. Seductively. Sexually. Shimmering. Shining. Effervescent. Desirable. Ann for a brief minute or two was a Tango Goddess and Ben wanted to pray at her altar. Ben couldn't believe it was just virtual. He so wanted to touch her.

All too soon, it was over. Ann said she was running out of juice but it was really the opposite, she had too much juice but there could be no coming back. If she wasn't careful, she would be violating the rules that enabled her to come down here. No matter how much one of them or both of them wanted it. Wanting it, is not the same as being able to get it and both of them were going to have to learn that lesson.

CHAPTER 31

THE DOOR BELL ONLY RINGS ONCE

The next morning, Ben was wakened by the sound of their doorbell. RRRING. Then again. RRING. Very few people used doorbells in Sedona. Instead guests would knock on doors or gesticulate in front of windows. They had one friend who explained the local practice as trying to avoid disturbing the Universe's Harmonic Forces. Fair enough.

Ben drew one of the window shades and to his surprise, he saw what he thought was a VERY small mid 90's Geo Metro in fire engine red. He was even more surprised to find Don (Yes, that Don) at the door. "He better not be on the run." Ben thought. He opened the door:

"What are you doing here? You didn't happen to meander from the prison, did you?" This was more likely than it might seem at first glance, because of the low key security features at a Federal Minimum Security Facility.} With Don though, one was always at risk from being along for a ride to in this case being CHARGED as an accessory. Given what had happened previously, Ben felt more than justified in asking.

"Nope, I'm free legitimately! My lawyer said I was free for good behavior pending the new trial."

"What happened?" Ben was still shocked that Don was here in Sedona.

"Something about fruit of the poisonous tree. Funny, I didn't know fruit could be dangerous. Vegetables maybe but not fruit. Apparently my employer had been illegally gathering evidence from my home phone in trying to track me down."

"Are you really going to have to go through a new trial?"

"My liar, I mean lawyer is hopeful that I can be a cooperating witness to detail what Gopher State executives did to try and collect their production bonuses no matter what it took. Maybe I won't have to do any more time in the slammer."

"But where are you HERE? Why aren't back home in Minneapolis with your wife?"

"She isn't home anyways. She's off helping her sick sister in Philly." Like Ben thought, the woman was a Saint.

Don continued: "After being cooped up in the Phoenix facility for almost a year, I thought it would be nice to drive back and see the country. Wanna come? We could work on my trial."

"But you already have an attorney."

"Not for much longer. My attorney is getting ready to bail if the Judge lets him. He hasn't been paid in 3 months. Gopher State had gotten all of our bank accounts frozen. At first my attorney wasn't too worried thinking My Go Fund Me page could cover it but my fifteen minutes of fame are far long gone and the fund is empty. We took out a second mortgage on our house for the first trial but there isn't enough equity left to tap that source again."

"So what are you going to do?"

Don stared at Ben for a moment and then answered, smiling: "The real question is what are you going to do about it? James, my attorney, said it would be a slam dunk after the evidence is thrown out. He said you probably won't even need to go to trial."

"So why can't he finish the slam dunk?" Attorneys almost never let go of an easy win.

"He runs a solo practice and can't afford it. Besides He has a major crime case going to trial in June."

"But I haven't done a criminal case in decades."

"It's like riding a bike, come on."

"I'll think it over."

Don smiled again for he knew it was only a matter of time before Ben gave in. Ben knew it too. After all, What are good friends for? Ben thought warily, he was soon to find out.

"Hey you still haven't answered my question about going on another road trip. This sweet ride is paid for and needs to be aired out."

In this case, the "sweet ride" was a rusty fire engine red 4 door Geo that Ben thought in his opinion would have to improve its safety record before it could be seen as a death trap. He wondered if the rust was holding it together. It looked less comfortable than a Yugo, another failed small import. He knew it was less comfortable, for Don had a similar Limeade colored Geo when they commuted in college so long ago. Guess he shouldn't have been so surprised that it was Don that pried himself out of it. Now Ben wondered how his older less flexible, long legs would be able to fit inside the car's "cabin." In college, Ben paid an extra $5 a week towards gas to avoid sitting in the back seat.

"Thanks but no thanks, I got things to deal with here."

"Got time for an early breakfast and hike?" It was still only 7:30 am.

"Does Amigos still have its early bird special on chicken fried steak?" Clearly, Don's diet had not improved since being in prison.

"Yep, though I'm not even supposed to look at anything fried. Let's go!" It was after all, almost 8 am when specials ended.

And with that they were off.

At Amigos, Ben went with the Huevos Rancheros while Don was finally able to satiate his alleged need for a chicken fried steak. For a guy who had been stuck in a 4 by 6 foot rental unit, Don did not look that bad. Then again, his outside might be covering up the danger within. Now that they had a proper food base, it was time to work off those calories, and talk things other to the extent it was possible.

Don asked if they could hike the Schnebly Hill Trail. It was a moderate hike about 5 miles and it would take 2.5 hours. Don had several 4 by 6 pictures of it that he asked Ben to send him in prison as a way of releasing his tension while Don's body remained caged. That hike sounded grand to Ben because to get there, once again the car would have to travel Hwy 179 all the way to the Y when the Highway split instead go up the hill. The vistas were so beautiful that they were used in auto and drug TV commercials. No Kidding.

It was still pretty early so they were surprised that the parking lot was almost full. They asked a very fit elderly woman who was carrying a large tube on her back what was going on. The woman asked them whether they had heard of the Plein (Not a typo-look it up.) Air Festival which celebrates painting outdoors and sure enough, at every vista there was at least 1 or 2 people setting up to enjoy the outdoors while they painted. It was great to see how many hardy seniors over age 75 that were there, enjoying their skills amid nature. Many still had a clear vision that was evident in the pictures they were painting. Don and Ben changed their mind and instead took the Marge Draws Trail which had the advantage of going by the Circle K store. No surprise, it was a beautiful hike. The Buttes and views at every turn. At the start they both stopped at the natural amphitheater to look at the back side of old Sedona and surrounding Buttes that looked next door but weren't. Next after crossing the hill road, they continued on the trail playing peek a boo with Magic Mountain and other famous Buttes. Don even spied Chimney Rock far off in the distance.

Don spent a lot of time talking about what he was going to do next. He had a lot of time to think about that while imprisoned. He wanted to make up for all that lost time with Deb and get a gig where he could work remotely. To Ben it sounded pretty sensible. Neither of them brought up Ann- leaving the situation as it was- whatever that was. By this time they were driving back to the Village of Oak Creek. They stopped at the Red Chopstick for lunch. They sat outside and stared at Bell Rock for a while. Neither said anything. Then, it was time for Don to drop Ben off and start the long way home. He wanted to make Albuquerque, New Mexico (originally named after some Spanish dude) before nightfall. It was good to see him and even better to see Don was on his way back to Minneapolis where he belonged.

Chapter 32

A Good Day for a Hike

The first phone text came in at 7am.

It said: I've got a Plaintiff's Steering Committee today in Phoenix. Already on the road. Want an overnight guest late this afternoon? We can catch up.

Ben: Always happy to see my favorite son. What is ETA?.

Larry: I think 5 or 6 pm. Gotta stop at phx office first. Will call or text if over 1.5 hr late.

Ben: You bringing a guest? Wanna grill?

Larry: No. Yes. Tx. Bye.

Ben: Travel safe. Bye to you also.

Bye to you also? He thought. What was it, though, that made parents act so lame in front of their kids? Ben closed his phone.

Their son, Larry was a very successful plaintiff's class action attorney in Los Angeles. Although, in the past, he tried cases mostly in Federal Court, he now filed many of his claims in California State Courts because the increasingly conservative Federal Courts were making it difficult for class actions to survive a summary judgment motion. (Legal talk for Judge ruling you lose and a party doesn't even get to argue their case in front of a jury.) So smart attorneys like Larry had already pivoted and filed their cases in a more favorable forum ie State Court. Both Ben and Ann were proud of him-he hoped his son knew that.

Larry was a champion multitasker in a good way. He always kept several plates, spinning all at once until they were all dry. He was probably coming into town, to meet with that big Phoenix law firm working on yet another big case. It only took 5 1/2 hours to drive from L.A. to Phoenix. Then, it was a straight shot up I-17 to their Sedona place. By the time you figured out the cost of getting to LAX airport and more importantly, the time in traffic jams/waiting in lines, it just made sense to drive.

Besides, Larry was taking more time for himself since his surgery. Ben hoped that Larry wasn't coming into Sedona just to talk about his mother-Ann again. He and Sissy were pretty close. Too close. Nosy sister-social worker, nosy son-attorney; it figured. He remembered that Larry had already set the groundwork by having his sister Sue call. Larry was crafty that way, coming at them from 2 different angles. (Sissy and Sue)

Rather than wait anxiously, all day around the house, he decided to go hiking and take some pictures. Ben was an avid P.P., phone photographer. He liked to make prints and put them in 2 buck IKEA frames. He had even sold some in what he called his art gallery but was just a plain old consignment store. He didn't have the time, money or talent to be in a gallery. Still, his budding photography career was going well until the consignment store went out of business with some of his framed photos. Of course, there was no phone or forwarding address. When he complained about it, one of his Sedona friends told him, the owner was just taking her free artistic license with artists, get used to it. Thinking about it, still made Ben stew, a little bit. Actually a lot. Is this how all artists are treated? No wonder Artists felt tortured. Too many people ripping them off. Anyways he could hit the grocery store on his way back from hiking.

He was in no rush. Ben had lots of time, too much time like all the retirees. Ben still consulted some, volunteered some, hiked some, took care of the house a little but there were still big gaping holes of excess time in every day. It had only gotten worse since Ann died. He didn't want to become addicted to internet or Netflix or Facebook. Some of their friends had.

When Ann was alive, it was different. She was a great partner and almost always willing to try anything. though she didn't get sports, at all. Art shows, car shows, last minute trips to Phoenix or Tucson and beyond. Overnight adventure trips, travels to different countries that he read about in history books, Ann was game especially to see or talk to her beloved grandkids. As a result, there was never enough time for all things that he and Ann wanted to do. Ben paused in the middle of the trail. After feeling sorry for himself for about 30 seconds, Ben got off the pity train and got ready to go.

That was one of the things Ben loved about hiking; you could be ready in a flash. When Ben had an extra hour or two, he would race to hike a trail.

He usually prepared quickly:

Filled water bladder? Check. (It looked like a small backpack with a plastic tube for ease of use.)

Poles? Check.

Boots? Check.

Juiced up phone? Check?

Snack? Check.

Sunglasses? Check.

Compass? He bought one but usually only remembered it after he had already left, directionless.

Map? On phone. Check.

In less than 5 minutes, he was ready to go.

Ben especially liked to hike and take photos in the early morning or late in the afternoon. That was when the sun was at its softest (morning) or truest (afternoon). Right before or after rain also was spectacular in that all the colors especially plants were rich. It was as if, they were giving thanks to their Creator.

Today, Ben decided to go to one of the quieter trails east of the village. Although he couldn't think of its name, he had a pretty good idea of where it was. He liked it because it had several different types of vistas: grassland trail, hilltop, river bottom and once he found the trail, it was difficult to get lost. (While everybody gets lost-here they call it getting misdirected, Ben had once gotten so lost by 179, he had to crawl underneath barbed wire and trespass several home owners' back yards to get back to the road. Thankfully, he didn't run into anyone he knew.) Still in general, it was a joyous activity and was healthy for him.

Ben also loved to take photos. He took a lot of them. An awful lot of them. Digital film was cheap. All right, it was free. He was amazed how different the same rocks could look at different times of the day or weather conditions. Castle Rock went from a dazzling gold in the morning around 8 am to a plain almost sandstone and then to a deep red then back to its gold close to 5 pm before later retreating in the dark. Ben had probably taken hundreds of pictures of Bob the Rock (Castle Rock) and he was nowhere near to being finished with taking them. While the Red Rocks were ever changing, they were also the same in some ways, much like life.

Ben parked near the church and then walked through the neighborhood to get to the trail. He started climbing and walked past the outdoor natural gas facility. Indeed, the trail for a while, started out above the buried gas line which probably explained the access to the public lands. He climbed up the rocky hill about 300 to 400 feet where the wild flowers liked to bloom in the spring. He turned to his right and beyond the Sedona Golf Resort, he could see the entire Village of Oak Creek.

Ben was so far away, the homes resembled little toasted bread croutons but he could easily make out Bell Rock, Lee Mountain and Courthouse Butte. He climbed further and he passed a little memorial to someone. It was a tin Cross sticking out of the ground with a dried flower bouquet nearby. Ben didn't know the story but somebody had clearly lost a loved one. He kept hiking avoiding the holes, rocks and thistle bushes that really, really dug deep. Though purple and pretty in spring, they spend most of the year just poking people.

He reached the crest of the hill and on the other side, it was a completely different physical environment. One of tall wavy golden grass. Totally different. He looked down the steep hill and saw a stream at its bottom and some distant cows drinking water in yet a third environment. He descended for a while and then stopped. Took a breath. Ben decided he didn't want to tucker himself out too early today with Larry coming there tonight.

At least, that was the excuse he used. He stopped back at the top and took some photos, took a long drink from his water bladder and ate his granola bar. It was grand. Then it was back the way he came with a couple stops to take pictures. Nice, real nice. And he hadn't come across a single person during his 2 ½ hour hike. Ben would have been hard pressed to tell you what he thought about while he hiked, but he was sure it must have been deep and relaxing. He sure felt good.

Afterwards, he walked back to the car and took another long swig from his water bladder. He supposed at this time of year, he could get by with just a large water bottle. In the summer, the water bladder was a necessity. So was hiking.

Chapter 33

Sue Calls

A call from Sue was always unexpected but never random. Ben had just settled down to nap when he phone rang. He was surprised to hear it was Sue again. Ben was even more surprised when she apologized for her last call:

"Sorry Dad, for my last call. It's just been so hard with everything we're going through."

Ben's body armor melted. Ann was right, he always was a softy when it came to their kids:

"I'm sorry too pumpkin. Anything I can do to help?"

"Nah, this is something we have to dig ourselves out of- you two have already been more than generous."

Wow, they were becoming self-reliant. Ben's only regret was that Ann wasn't there to hear it.

"Listen Dad, I just wanna be sure you're ok. I have to admit I was more than a little freaked when I heard you were hearing Mom again. You're not hearing anybody else, are you?"

"Unless you're talking about Winston Churchill, Nope. (Ben, history buff had long been a student of World War Two) Just kidding."

"I care about you, Pops."

"I care about you too."

"Gotta get back to my job. Listen if it works for you, it'll work for me too. I just need some time to get used to it." And then she hung up. More softly this time.

The glow that Ben felt lasted for hours. No parent stops loving their kids. Well, almost no one. Parents might get frustrated, disappointed, angry with their progeny, hope still resides somewhere within the heart. That old "Hope Springs Eternal" stuff. Whatever. The important thing was- Sue was doing better. A lot better. How this happened or why it occurred, he might never know. Ann might- he was going to ask her. Ben felt he and Ann were lucky. Many parents weren't. Ben hoped he and Ann let the kids know often enough how they felt about them.

CHAPTER 34

LARRY COMES AROUND

Then it was time to go to the grocery store where they claimed to have everything you needed and more. While they had a nice take out deli, expresso coffee, gelato, thoughtful wine and spirits, Ben had come for some fresh steaks and a salad. He also picked up both a red and white wine so he was covered with whatever Larry wanted. That's what parents do. For dessert, Ben picked some premium sorbet (See, he was trying to do better on the calorie count.) and he was good to go.

He was home in 2 minutes and again, yep, that's one of the advantages from living in a suburb that appears to have landed in a National Park. He got home, changed out of his clothes, took a shower to eliminate the dust and after wondering where Ann was, promptly fell asleep listening to the cable news in his under wear.

Napping seemed to be a new hobby for Ben. He did it almost every day. Unlike Don who would qualify for the Sleep Olympics, Ben only napped after hiking or in the midafternoon. He supposed it was partially due to the fact he wasn't sleeping through the night, but his sleep was getting better with Ann being back and getting some exercise.

Still, he felt he had a large sleep deficient probably due to grief. It was going to take a while, before things got back to normal, whatever that new normal was.

He woke up an hour later, about 11 am and decided to have a grilled cheese sandwich (Velveeta) and Tomato soup (Campbell's). Ben liked to get his salt and preservatives from professionals.

Ann POPPED in just as he was about to sit down to eat.

"Got a spare bowl of soup? Except for the Velveeta, that almost looks like a real meal." Ben had put out veggies too, to nibble on.

"Hey, nice to see you, too, why the late start?"

"To be honest, that was quite the night and it took a lot out of me."

"I'm not surprised. You were an unforgettable Tango dancer last night. I loved it. Can we do that again? Like maybe Tomorrow?"

"Down boy. Someday, a maybe for a birthday." Ann felt they had both come too close to breaking the rules whatever they were. She wasn't gonna let that happen again.

"Well, it's already been a good day. I went hiking and Larry is coming to spend the night at 6 pm."

"That's great! How's he feeling?"

"I couldn't ask. We only texted. You know Larry- he's a man of few characters, at least on texting. I'll find out how's he's feeling tonight."

"Just don't push him. You know how much he hates that. And if you can, it would be interesting to find out if he's seeing any one. I'm more than curious."

"Nice to see you're interested in someone else's personal life other than mine. Now that you mention it, Ann you do look a little faded, are you OK?"

"I still need a little rest if I want to stop by and stay tonight. Even if I can't talk to Larry, I can at least see and listen to him. I better leave now to get charged up." Without waiting for answer, she weakly POPPED and was gone.

Ben spent the afternoon reading his John Le Carre spy novel. He had probably read it before but he wasn't sure. He hated it when he would get half way through a book, only to find he had read it before. John Le Carre was an excellent writer who wrote about the moral ambiguity in our lives. Maybe he should go back to Jack London, very little ambiguity there. (Truly, dog eat dog in his books like White Fang.)

What he really should have done is work on his writing projects but he didn't feel like it. Ben had two Arbitration Awards to write and his novel to work on. Retirement could end up being a lot of work if a person wasn't careful.

When Ann was physically around, he would get up early at 3 am to write for 2 or 3 hours before she got up. That way they could spend the day together. In addition, Ann was a great sounding board and editor. But now, with Ann gone, he had to get himself going, and keep it going. Writing can be trying- at times tedious, solitary pursuit. Maybe that's why so many writers get started early in the day- to get it out of the way.

He still did his most productive writing early in the day but without getting much sleep, it was just more and more difficult to get up early. It sounded like an excuse but it was true. Things had gotten a lot better since Ann returned.

It was funny that the legal writing didn't seem to take the same amount of physical/emotional energy that his creative fiction writing did. Sometimes, it was plain exhausting. He had been working on a murder mystery that takes place in a housing cooperative that closely resembled where he and Ann had lived. Like a condo building but with different ownership structure- buildings were usually older and quirkier. He had been working on it for 2 years and wasn't getting anywhere after writing 100 pages.

At 5 pm, he turned on the local Phoenix news and at 5:30, he switched to national news. In Sedona they got cable because otherwise with the Rocks, they couldn't receive anything.

He heard a car door slam softly, more like a thunk and their son Larry had arrived in his red model S Tesla. It was a remarkable car and Larry was so happy with it, that he bought it outright when his original lease expired. It reminded Ben of a panther. It was silent going forward like all electric cars and it had incredible torque. It would really knock a passenger instantly back into their car seat when the driver stepped on the gas, rather, the acceleration pedal. But what amazed Ben the most, was the outstanding fit and finish of the car built by a company that did not exist 20 years ago.

Larry wearing a long sleeved shirt and tie, walked up to the door, holding an overnight bag. He was tall, dark and handsome.

At age 31, all his mother wanted to know was why he was still single. Ben noticed her sitting in the corner of the living room. He didn't know how long she had been sitting, or floating there depending on your point of view.

"Larry (He didn't like being called son) good to see you, how was the drive?"

"Not bad Ben, (No surprise there, he hadn't called him Dad since age 15), I got out of Phoenix by 3:30 but there was a truck rollover on I-17 going up. It delayed me by an hour."

"Well, I'm really glad you're here, we can catch up."

"Yep"

"You look tired. You doing OK?"

"I'm fine, don't worry. Please stop asking. I just had my 2 year post surgery checkup and I am still cancer free."

"That's something to celebrate. Why don't you put your stuff in the second bedroom while I start the bbq coals. (Larry was old school- no natural gas or propane heat for their meat) There's beer or wine in the fridge if you want it."

"Sounds good." Larry turned, grabbed a beer and walked into the bedroom. He shut the door. Larry still shut them out, sometimes. It was just like high school, all over again. Caring but not always sharing.

Chapter 35

Ben and Larry Talk-Almost

Ben started the charcoal. He used both pre lit coals and plenty of lighter fluid, because as he figured, why take chances? Whoosh, the fire started nicely, just 20 minutes and they could start cooking those thick steaks.

Ann walked through the screen and sat down, she was wearing a pink jump suit with a pretty blue coral necklace.

"He looks good, but tired. That's great about being cancer free for 2 years. Too bad he's been relationship free for 2 years also. Now, if he could only work on meeting someone."

"Can't you just let him figure it out?"

"Well, he hasn't."

"Talk about being pushy."

"I'm not being pushy, I'm just being.."

Just then the screen door opened. Larry, wearing a grey short sleeved shirt, walked through carrying two opened beers.

"I thought I heard you speaking to someone."

"No, I was just mumbling to myself."

"Want a beer?"

"Sure, thanks for asking." Ben took one of the Oak Creek Amber beers, toasted Larry and then asked how things were going.

"Pretty well, in fact. I was in Phoenix discussing a new potential case with Glassman and Stissle. It's a class action involving 1.7 million plaintiffs in California alone. The other big state is Arizona with 1.1 million potential claimants and they've agreed to pony up to $1 million in costs. It's a financial fraud case. It's a big deal." (Larry never exaggerated on his numbers, if he said it was big, it was.)

Ben was a little envious. He never got to play in the big sandbox. Not many lawyers did. Still, he was happy for his son.

"That's great news." Then Ben noticed Ann strongly signaling him. She was gesticulating so wildly Ben was afraid she would dislocate her shoulder. He didn't think Spirits could have that happen, virtual or not: "So what's new on the social front? Seeing anyone?" Ann would have definitively handled it better. But what could she expect from a non-mother?

"Gosh you just sound like Mom. Can't you just give it a break?"

Ben glared at Ann, then spoke:

"I'm sorry..talk to your sisters lately?

"No not really, but I have spoken to Fran." This was not good.

"She confirmed you've been talking with Mom again."

"I told you about it in a phone call, already"

"I thought it was just once in a while. Fran said this could be the start of a major psychosis."

This was worse.

"She also said that Don got arrested in Arizona for Bank Fraud, is this true?"

"Sort of.."

"Finally, she said you broke Don's nose on the drive down there."

"Maybe. If I did, he certainly deserved it."

"Boy, you three have been busy…"

"I can explain.."

"No Dad, you listen. You remember what happened last time you were hearing voices. This time, you broke Don's nose and he ends up in jail. I know I promised not to do anything but, come on, man!" It was more a plea than a yell.

"What are you going to do, put me on a time out, every time I speak to your Mom?"

"Is she here right now? Are you hearing more than one voice?"

Ann had floated off for a minute so the first answer was no. Ben was not hearing voices, rather only one voice so that answer was no also.

"No and No. Let's change the subject. How about a nice juicy steak and salad? Can we pick it up tomorrow and cut each other some slack?"

"Ok but we're not done talking."

"I'm sure we will never be."

The rest of the night with Larry passed pleasantly enough. They talked about easy stuff-old family vacations and what his friends were up to. As long as the topic of Ann didn't come up, they were fine. Ben enjoyed middle aged Larry, a lot more than teen age Larry.

Teenage Larry was a pill that Ben could never swallow. Larry was always angry. Always. Not like he was yelling or anything but more like a sullen silence that hovered over the house like a dark grey rain cloud. But why shouldn't he be- Ben was the same way in his younger years. His parents were mostly afraid of him and tried to avoid direct meaningful communication. As a result, Ben tried to be the exact opposite with his son. Ben tried to take an interest in Larry's life (read parental interference), provide some direction (read more parental interference), and most irritating of all to Larry- Ben tried to promote healthier habits as helpful suggestions as in: "You getting enough sleep?" and "Won't playing the music that loud damage your ears?" Ann had it easier, she gave less advice and as a result received fewer glares. Still with the passage of time and Ben learning to keep his mouth shut more often, Ben and Larry had a better relationship. Especially since Ann died. Not necessarily closer but better.

With his surgery, Larry was trying to take better care of himself, too, so it was no surprise that Larry begged off at 9:30 pm.

"Sorry pops, but I'm beat. I've been up since 4:30 am. I've got to get some sleep. Sorry, if I got so harsh about mom. We'll figure something out. Let's leave it alone for a while."

"Deal. Wanna hike Bell Rock Trail at 7:30 am before you leave?"

"Wish I could, but I'm taking a deposition at 3 pm in LA." (Larry was a busy, busy guy.) And with that Larry shuffled off to bed. When he was this tired, Larry almost looked like an old man. Ben stayed outside to talk to Ann who had reappeared.

Ann had been sitting patiently, drinking in all she could of her only son. She was pleased.

"He's doing ok."

"We did more than ok.

"We did great except for you pushing him."

"You told me to, besides why do you always take his side?"

"Isn't it obvious? He's my son-I gave birth to him. He's part of me. You-I just married. Son always trumps husband. Anyways, ready to call it a night?"

"Almost." Ben grabbed another beer.

"Can I see you in the morning?

"You betcha." POP and she was gone.

Ben stayed out a bit longer and stared at the stars. They seemed to be winking at him. Or maybe it was the cloud cover passing by. He was a mostly lucky man. He went inside and planned to sleep deeply until 7 am.

Chapter 36

A Little Night Magic

But that wasn't meant to be. When you're part of a couple, even when one of you isn't alive, you only sleep as well as the lightest sleeper. Ann slept no better after death than she did in life which is to say not much. "Why sleep when you can fret?" was something she liked to say to Ben. But tonight she had something better in mind. It was the first Wednesday of the month and as a result it was "Over the Hump Day" and Spirits shared Happy Hour. Holding the party over Mount Everest gave Over the Hump, a whole new meaning and Ann loved the special effect lightning shows that were put on. Ann had been planning on taking Ben there for some time but something always seemed to come up. But tonight was going to be different. Ann was determined to bring Ben here and talk over big things. She needed Ben to be in a good mood and figured lack of sleep couldn't hurt. At first she thought another saucy dance session might work but she didn't want to risk her or Ben's status. Plus that night of dancing took a lot out of her and she had some important things to talk about. But first she had to wake him up, successfully. This wasn't always easy. Wake him up too hard, he was cranky. Too softly, he would simply roll over and fall back to sleep. That, too, could be a problem. Ann once woke up Ben or so she thought, so he could drive her to work during a snow storm. Unfortunately, Ben was not really awake and drove her car into a brick wall. It caused $4600 damage to the car but no one was hurt. Apparently, there really is a potentially dangerous and expensive malady called sleep driving.

"Ben, honey... (Sometimes sweet endearments helped, the sweeter the better to release more endorphins.) Time to get up."

"Huh? What time is it?"

"It's long past time to get up. I've got a surprise for you."

"Can it wait for breakfast?"

"Come on Big Guy, you've always loved Happy Hour. I'm gonna take you to one that's out of this world."

"Is there a free buffet like Chi-Chi's?" Ben rolled over to his right. This meant he was waking up. He looked at his watch with only one eye open, as per his normal practice. That way he figured he had only one eye awake and he could fall back asleep easier: "Hey, it's only 2 am."

Ann was getting impatient: "I don't care, we gotta get going. You get up right now."

"But its 3 am..." Ben had managed to locate his left arm and looked at his watch.

"Look, I went to a lot of trouble to get you invited and you are not going to be blow this off like you did the American Association of University Women Fundraiser."

| 233

Even after 17 years, Ann still maintained righteous indignation over Ben's claiming a migraine and then sneaking off to a poker game while she went to the fundraiser alone where she was handing out the Thrifty Woman Scholarship that year.

In Ben's defense that dinner was usually, alright always, a snooze fest and in spite of his napping he would still have had a migraine by the time he got home.

"Come on, there's a light show and you might be able to see your parents." This meeting was important to Ann. After all, her Spiritual Leader was advising her that it was long past time for her to be hanging around her husband. She was advised that if she waited too long, he would never be able to move on with his life or meet someone new.

Anne had her own reasons for wanting Ben to be able to move on. Selfish but understandable reasons.

While Anne cared deeply about Ben's happiness, Anne was even more concerned about getting someone to serve as an appropriate Bubbe (Grandma). Her son was finally at a place in his life where the thought of having a child or two didn't automatically make him gag. But someone had to be around do the heavy lifting as the beloved grandma. Ben was a great husband but like most of them, he just couldn't successfully do it all on his own. Anne believed he still didn't understand when a diaper needed to be changed or that you could and he did, put them on backwards when their children were babies. Left unsupervised, he probably still would. And who knows, maybe her son, Larry, would name the kid after her. That would be great and well deserved in her not so modest opinion.

Ben sat up. Immediately.

"Is that really possible? How would that work?"

"Well, it involves reversing the polarity of matching vortexes with memories, suffice it to say it is complicated and very technical." Sometimes, Ann liked to show off. It must be the AAUW sheen rubbing off on her. "I'm sorry but you'll only be able to see them, not talk to them."

"Heck, that's something. I'd love to. It's been so long since they passed on that it's getting harder to remember what they looked like. This will at least refresh my memory" Like many people, Ben didn't like saying his parents had died (It hit too close to home.) and instead used euphemisms like: passed, gone to the other side, on the other side of the grass, etc. It allegedly hurt less that way. Ben found it didn't really work.

"Trust me, I know how you feel."

Ben got dressed quickly now. "Thanks for setting this up."

Ann blinked twice and with a soft POP, (after all it was 315 am) they were gone.

A couple of seconds and a couple thousands of miles later, they were at Happy Hour in the clouds.

To Ben, it looked like a cross between Club Med and the steam bath at the Jewish Community Center of Minneapolis. There was a soft moist level of steam about 3 inches above their feet. Everybody was shoeless and clothing was optional. Like, the J.C.C Men's Steam Baths, men's body shape was inversely proportional to whether they wore clothing. In other words, the younger and better looking a Spirit was, the more likely they would be wearing a white yet tasteful athletic track outfit. Ben tried unsuccessfully, not to look. The older balding men were almost all naked in spite of their dangling participles. They must be figuring that they had nothing to lose except their self-respect and apparently they didn't care about that either. Ben definitely didn't want to look there at their withering stalks. Relieved that he found he was still dressed, Ben thought a change of topic and view would be a good idea:

"Say, where are all the ladies?"

"Sorry Tiger, but its Mah Jong Game Night at the Women's Spa. It's a converted YWCA facility. Still needs a little work. All those foggy days on Earth? It's our steam bath overheating. Still we're pleased with it. We got tired of all the male Spirits lurking and leering at us. So we got our own little piece of Heaven. Why do you think I brought you up on a Tuesday?"

"What's with the no shoe gambit?"

"You think earth is the only place guests have to take their shoes off when they come inside?" Ann answered arching an eyebrow. "These clouds get dirty very easily and they're Hell to clean. Pretty tough to scrub a cloud." Wow. Some people never changed no matter where they were. Ann had always been a fanatic about keeping her surface areas clean. She even kept a couple extra pairs of slippers at their house for guests who felt foolish wandering the halls with just their socks on. (This apparently ran in her family. Ann's mother had all the living furniture encased in that old thick plastic that stuck to your legs during hot summer days.)

"Makes sense." Ben looked out of the corner of his eye and saw several older men sword fighting with multicolored light sabers. Thankfully, these Spirits were all wearing clothes. Funny, Star Wars was still big, even up here.

"Can I play?" asked Ben. He was truly star struck and there was a crowd of 15 to 20 Spirits, mostly male, watching the match.

"Sorry, there's a required sign up. People wait weeks for their turn". Ann answered. "Besides this is a fundraiser for the Star Maker Alliance."

"Huh. Ok." Ben mumbled in agreement, even though he didn't have a clue as to what Ann was talking about. Ben often said that when he didn't know what to say or wasn't paying attention. Tonight he definitely was paying attention but it was a lot to take in. An awful lot. Ann reminded herself to be patient.

"I gotta admit this is pretty cool." Ben was looking across the cloud where he now saw several couples slow dancing and a couple of people playing chess. It reminded him of a Halloween Sigma Alpha Sigma College Fraternity Party where they had placed dry ice in water to give off this same cloudy other worldly effect.

"When am I going to be able to see my parents?'

"Look over there." Ann pointed to a domestic scene that emerged from a rotating cloud. There were two Spirits with smaller clouds at their feet. It was Ben's parents! Wow, Ben thought. It looked like a typical after dinner evening scene with Ben's Mom knitting while watching TV and his father reading the afternoon newspaper.

"They look content." Ben was pleased for it brought back a rush of memories of his parents.

"They ARE content." Ann answered.

"I wish we could have had a lot more evenings like that. They and you were gone too soon."

"I feel the same way." The cloud with Ben's parents turned slowly and started floating away.

"Hey! I wasn't ready for them to go. I'm still not. Can't I talk to them?"

"Sorry, it isn't possible."

Ben felt his cheeks get wet. Was it his tears? He didn't know.

"No one ever is. Listen, I wanted to talk to you about our son Larry." Ann was ready to change the topic. Although they both had participated in the design and formation of Larry, Ann was much more personally invested in Larry's future.

"Ok, what's up?"

"I think he's going to get married next summer."

"How do you know? Got any inside information?" It seemed to Ben that Mothers sometime did have an inside track and intuition as to their children's whereabouts and needs of the progeny even if Larry didn't know them yet. Must be a more highly developed version of maternal ESP. Like many mothers, Ann didn't like to talk about it.

"A Mother just knows. His cancer really shook him up. He's got a better appreciation now of time passing. Like all of us, his body clock only runs in one direction and he's not getting any younger."

"I suppose that's good but what's the big deal?"

"I believe they're gonna have children."

"That's even better than having one child, isn't it?" Ben was confused. Children meant a family future. Progeny. Posterity or was it Prosperity? Circle of Life and all that stuff. Ben sometimes got confused about these issues. But Ann? Never. So far, all she had talked about were things they wanted to happen. Things the couple had dreamed about, talked about. But sometimes Ben's dreams for Larry were not as highly evolved as Ann's. Must come from the same part of the brain where maternal ESP comes from. Ann would at times get more than a little frustrated that Ben could not keep up.

Sometimes, men are so clueless: "You gotta start thinking about some changes in your life, too."

"Why? I like the way things are."

Typical: "You can't keep on living like this."

"Why not? In spite of you're not living - we've never gotten along so well." Ben thought he was showing how flexible he was and that he had adjusted to this admittedly, unusual situation. Ann's next words put a kibosh on Ben's laisse faire attitude to the current situation.

"I'm not gonna be here forever."

"Why not?"

"Aren't you lonely?"

"No, why should I be? I got you, Babe."

Unbelievable. Like many guys, he still thought that song was still a clever line. Ann wondered if the Estate of Sonny and Cher received premium pay every time a middle aged man sang "I Got You Babe" in falsetto like Ben just did. Ann sure hoped so.

"It's not the same. Look, your life is not one big bagel. That hole in your heart is no longer doing you any good."

Ann shook her head. She was getting frustrated. This wasn't getting anywhere. Her supervisor was right, she had to get out of there so Ben could heal and really move on. By now, he should have enough scar tissue. He would never be able to meet someone if she was lurking around (her word choice not mine). You can't spend all of your present just living in the past.

"Let's pick this up tomorrow." Ann sighed. Her mentor was right. This wasn't going to be easy.

"Hey, we haven't even played ping pong yet." Ben like most men was easily distracted and was watching 2 Spirits playing Ping-Pong without paddles. Huh, must be mind control. He thought some more.

"Can't we take that world cruise we talked about but could never afford?"

"Still can't afford it- Too high of a price. I'd have to save energy for months to save up and you wouldn't be able to see or hear me while I was scrimping and saving." Ann had had always been the practical one of the two. She balanced their checkbook. (Remember those?) and paid the bills. She shuddered to think of how Ben was now, unsupervised, handling that stuff.

"Ok, then, what about the Light Show, you promised?"

"All right, 2 minutes tops." It was like negotiating with a 12 year old, make that a 10 year old. No request was ever the final one. They always wanted more.

Ann gave a small wave and the sky above them (what else could you call it?) starting turning darker and then slowly different hues appeared- red, yellow, green like a celestial slide show. It was as if Ann had taken a rainbow and spread out the colors one at a time. It was beautiful. It was awesome. It was also time to go.

"Come on partner, time to get you home."

Ben didn't want to go back home. Yet. He tried his almost patented basketball Stall Shot:

"Hey, I never got to try any of the snacks up here." Ben felt it wasn't fair that he was being cheated again. Most 10 year old boys could sympathize with his self-anointed unfair predicament. But sadly, his weak effort bounced off an imaginary rim.

Ben had always been like this at the Minnesota State Fair. There was always one more ride, one more exhibit, one more deep fat fried food that had to be savored and stretched out. And he always, always had to ride the Space Tower right before they went home. There was something soothing and exciting about going slowly up 300 feet and seeing a 360 degree view as it rotated. It was magnificent. Why, it was a family tradition. They had no choice. Well, tonight Ann did.

Ann POPPED her charge back to his bed. Maybe a little too hard. Ben bounced off the bed like an overdone Pop Tart and hit the floor. Hard. Miraculously, he did not wake up. In a sleep depraved slumber, he simply picked himself up and deposited his body back in bed.

Huh, you don't always hurt the one you love. But sometimes you do. Sometimes, you need to.

In any case, Ann had more than enough of his whining for one night. Tomorrow was another day. Maybe her final one.

CHAPTER 37

ALMOST BUT NOT QUITE THERE

It was another beautiful day in Sedona. It was a bright blue, no, a spectacular blue. No Clouds yet. Ben wished he could take a picture that detailed, not just the color, but the feeling of it: sidewalk chalk blue. Artists sometimes call it Cobalt Blue.

The Clouds, puffs of cotton, lazily floated by like they were lounging on an invisible air mattress in a backyard pool.

Ben felt the trails definitely calling to him, he dressed quickly and then he walked to the kitchen for a cup of coffee. He had a strange dream last night and he wanted his coffee to tether him to earth. Had he really had his head and the rest of himself in the clouds with Ann, last night? Gosh, those light sabers were cool. He looked around and didn't see Larry.

Larry had gotten up and left at 6:00 am. He left a post it note on the microwave that said he wanted to beat rush hour traffic in Phoenix and LA but he promised to be back soon. He was still sorry about what he said. We can talk later, the note ended.

In the sunroom, there Ann was standing majestic, arms on hips, wearing a beautiful, multicolored Japanese Kimono:

"We raised a good man but right now we need to talk. It's time, Ben." She paused: "Not to let go but to move on."

Ben thought hard for a moment, then asked:

"Huh, what does that mean?" Ben worried a bit, was she dumping him for some younger Spirit in the Sky? He hadn't even been given the courtesy of finishing a first cup of coffee. But when Ann wanted to talk, they talked.

"It's time. Rather simple, really. I think you are ready…"

"Ready for what?"

"Getting on with your life.."

"But, I'm still not ready."

"Gonna have to be."

"Why?"

"Because I said so." Ann shook her head. This type of logic had never worked on her children and was unlikely to work on Ben.

"But what about us?"

"We will always have Sedona, just kidding, sorry- we will always have each other. You know that. You've always known that. No one can take that away. But Time isn't waiting, it never does. It's time for you to catch up to your life and move on"

Ben wasn't happy. He pouted:

"Were you ever, really here? I wanna know. I need to know."

"I don't truthfully know. What do you think?"

Ben looked down at his fingernails, he was embarrassed. At first, he didn't know why. How can you ever tell your beloved babe, who looks that great in a kimono that she may or may not exist?

"I like to think you were or still are…" Lately he'd been having beginnings of doubts, even when they were talking.

"Benny, like I told you, I will always be nearby- in your heart. I'm not going anywhere. I'll be around. Promise. I just won't be showing up as often. You are healing…"

"But I will miss you a lot." Benny was sure about this.

"Don't worry-I'll be showing up in your memories as much as you like. In addition, we can replay those memories in full 3D color dreams. What the hell, we can even have some passionate nights, complete with 1980's Barry Manilow music! If you watch what you eat better, I might even spring for some appetizers."

"I'm still not sure about this…" Though appetizers did sound good. Ben wondered if he could talk her into a fried onion blossom.

"You don't have to be… Look, your heart is now strong enough. Over time, it will get even stronger. Just don't do anything stupid with Don when he gets off probation. Otherwise, I might have to POP back in for supervisory and disciplinary purposes."

"I like the part about you coming back."

"I figured that. I love you, Ben, always have. I always will. Bye."

"Love you, too."

Ann POPPED, quite loudly this time, and she was gone. For good, it seemed. Funny, how things work out that way.

Ben finished his now, cold coffee, and exhaled a heavy sigh, full of love, longing and happy memories. He looked outside and saw a large cloud slowly move behind Bob the Rock, Could it be…Nah, Ben decided. He felt the trails calling him.

He wondered where he had left his hiking boots. Ann would know…she always did. He sighed again, this time, the sigh didn't feel as good. Almost a pain in his heart, an ache really. Still he got up and started looking for his shoes. It was long past time… to start moving on.

Ben found the boots on his own, finally (Like most middle aged men, he really could manage when he put his mind to it), and laced them up. Slowly. Firmly. Walking outside, he saw a single, solitary Cloud hovering over the nearby Butte for a minute, then watched as it slowly moved beyond the large rock. Almost like it was taking a leisurely walk. Not a bad idea.

Ben still didn't know about what Spirits do but he thought maybe people should, too. That is: Move On. So he grabbed his hiking poles and strode purposefully ahead. Ben didn't look back. Neither did the Cloud.

So instead, it followed him as Ben followed the curvy course of 179. Funny that there didn't seem to be other clouds out today, maybe they were taking their C.E.C. (Cloud Education Credits) or maybe they were just hanging out somewhere else. Ben could tell the remaining, solitary cloud was following him as he occasionally glanced through the moon roof of the car. Like an errant child, it darted in and out of view. It was comforting in a way.

Was Ann keeping an eye on him? Ben didn't know but didn't want to rule it out. He drove passed the entrance for Bell Rock Trail that was already full of cars. It looked to be a crisp day for hiking and the car noted the outside temperature was 43 degrees Fahrenheit. Brisk, meant he would walk faster. Was supposed to get up to 57 degrees. He passed a couple more trail heads then the Temple. After he passed the roundabout for the Cathedral Rock, his mouth eased into a grin- he knew he wasn't far now. (Ben would have liked to hike Cathedral Rock but it was just too popular with the masses yearning to connect with the alleged vortex forces. The Forest Service had given up trying to develop adequate parking and instead resorted to parking tickets to the cars that parked on the narrow road.)

Ben passed a couple of swanky resorts, all the time admiring the view, and before he knew it, he was at the turn off of Marge Daws Trail. He parked the car at the trail head. Only one car there. Good, if he had driven up further

| 247

to the other end of the hike up on Schnebly Hill, he would have found 10 to 15 cars already there. He had been introduced to the trail like many others by Joy but her hiking days were long gone. Her legs could no longer handle the climbing. Too bad, he thought although he was glad she was realistic on her limits. Not all people are. The key is reaching a realistic truce with your advancing age, not to just give in and give up. People like Joy, Freada and Marv were great mentors. Ben was grateful for that. He hoped he and Ann let them know it. Gratitude is underutilized until it's too late. Gotta thank people while you can. This is another part of life that you just don't get a do over.

Ben pulled his poles out of the car and checked his boots one final time. He grabbed his water and he was off. The first 200 hundred feet and stairs were the most difficult. The stairs started by being too long, (i.e. too far apart) and they prevented an easy gait going up. Then the stairs become extremely steep, at least 2 feet for each stair. Ben was glad he had his poles. They made the impossible, possible. In any case, after a sharp upwards curve to avoid a tree that had exposed roots and seemed to be hanging on for dear life, he was up on the plateau. Now Ben could turn around and take in the view.

It was a beautiful sight. Ben never tired of it. Although the checkerboard of townhomes and multi-million dollar houses marred the view a little, Ben didn't really mind. The cloud had disappeared again. The Buttes and Sedona could be seen in the distance. After about 997 pictures of this vista, Ben was finally, learning to just breathe in and enjoy the view.

Then he turned back to the trail and looked at the cacti. It had been a while since he had been on the trail and the cacti rot had only gotten worse. Cacti eating disease and varmints all loved to eat what Ben thought was a hardy plant protected by thorns. Several Obvious lessons in that. In the end, the cacti turn grey, cuddle up within themselves and die. As do we all. "Knock it off." Ben said to himself. "It's too early and too beautiful to be getting so heavy in the beginning of day." Suitably chastised, Ben got back to the trail. It was a meandering path straight east until he reached the T. He couldn't resist turning back every now and then and still only the magic mountain shone back at him. At this part of the day, it was a bright gold color. After about 20 minutes, after the sun moved, it would go back to a majestic grey-red- brown. Ben didn't really know the colors, he just knew he liked it and that was enough for him.

He started thinking about his writing. Weighing heavy on him. Sigh. Again. Still wasn't getting any further on his projects. The arbitration awards at least had a deadline date, but his novels only had his daily writing goal of 1,000 words a day and a vague notion of when he wanted to be done. Many professional writers like Stephan King managed to churn out 2,000 words a day while serious writers like Ernest Hemingway managed at least 500. Sarah Waters wrote 1000 and admitted many of those were still initially rubbish. Ben reminded himself that 900, alright 600 words would still be a vast improvement from what he was doing now. He was impressed with the diligence of writers who undertook the difficult, solitary vocation of writing.

But who could write today when it was so gorgeous out? Not Ben. Nope, give him a trail, a path, a sidewalk anything was an excuse to walk and explore. Even if he had been there 1,000 times before. Ben found the hiking to be a great time to focus. That's what he was doing right now- focusing. Keep the house (for at least another year), making his writing more of a priority- all of this made sense as inspirational and perspirational goals.

By this time, he had made it to Schnebly Hill. He walked across the lane and up the trail til he reached the parking lot. Yep, 9:15 am and it was almost already full. Feeling vindicated, why he didn't know, he still stopped at the vista point on the way back to the crossing. The buttes even though they were closer, looked further away. Must be the angle. Or maybe yet another vortex? Ben wondered what the plural of vortex was, vorti? Magic Mountain (At least that's what he called it) still looked majestic but from this vantage point, he couldn't see Chimney Rock. Strange when he looked at them earlier, they appeared to be right next to each other.

Ben took a deep breath, still wished Ann were here, and tried to push the pain in his heart away by starting on the trail back. He had just started a descent into what appeared to be a small empty waterfall of a dry seasonal stream bed when his foot encountered the pebble with his name on it. His legs flipped up to the sky suddenly and he found himself a minute later sprawled on the ground off the trail and in pain. Ben's ankle seemed at least twisted and there were abrasions on his face. This was a good thing for as experienced climbers will advise, you always want to fall forward. Faces, surgeons can fix but brain injuries to the back of the head? Not so much. Ben hoped he hadn't broken his ankle. And after all that yogurt he was eating- maybe that would help.

Still, Ben must have fallen hard because his unbreakable glasses were bent and there were contusions on his face that were bleeding. There was also the disgusting sense that he had inhaled a large amount of Red Rock dust. He found some old tissue in his pocket and blew his nose. Everything connected to his body seemed to be working. He unbent his glasses put them on and realized how lucky he was- another 18 inches and he could have gone over the waterfall edge. Several hikers died each years from falls, hypothermia and the occasional heart attack from over exertion. Some may have even "fallen" on purpose. But what a pretty way to go. Still Ben wasn't ready yet to let go. He still had a lot of hikes left in those boots. He felt that strongly. Besides, Ben had promised Ann, he wouldn't do anything stupid. Especially not when he had adult children to annoy on behalf of both of them.

Ben finally looked up after spitting out some more red dust and saw the Cloud had returned. Still solitary. It wasn't as puffy as before. Now, more like candy floss just pulled off the paper cone. Was it possible? Nah, it couldn't be her. But then, you just never know. He sure hoped so. Ben knew he would carry Ann in his heart forever. Maybe Ann was right, with the passage of time there would be more pleasurable memories and less heart ache. Maybe not. Still the Cloud drifted off again. Moving slowly with clear intent. But then so was Ben. He stood up, dusted himself off and leaned more heavily on his poles. Then he started gingerly, like we all should after a fall and possible injury. Walking, more like- hobbling back to his car. One painful step at a time. Step. Step. Breathe. Step… Like all of us, Ben still had some new trails to explore. Even as he continued to feel that heavy ache in his heart and current pain in his ankle. His, maybe their journey wasn't over. Not by a long shot.

Always.

Move.

Forward.

The End.

Author's Note

The month my parents both died, 30 plus years ago, was a very painful experience for everyone in our immediate family. We had not, expected not one, no less two, of our parents slipping from this earth in such a short time (Both in less than 30 days from each other), so unexpectedly. For months, I couldn't talk to anyone about it except my wife Barb who was incredibly, but not surprisingly, to anyone who knows her, very supportive.

In the first few months after their death, I would thereafter for several months, see my mom in a busy crowd, on occasion, and when I looked again, she would be gone. This went on for several montha until she stopped "showing up". I knew she hadn't been there but my eyes saw what they saw. After doing some research, I found my experience was not uncommon. (For example, a study showed, 30% of widowed seniors' experience, what is called bereavement hallucinations- hearing or seeing a loved one after they die.) That feeling was a partial starting point for this novel. See also Oliver Sacks M.D. in his book: Hallucinations.

We all suffer painful losses, and most of the time, given enough space, we can heal. Even when we don't know how the deep the scars are or what exactly will relieve our pain. Time can be a healer- not always great but it may heal or allow the growth of enough scar tissue to carry on. And who knows, maybe a remnant of a Spirit or loved one lives on- in the slow moving clouds, or in the whispering winds, or rustling of the leaves. Perhaps, maybe, just maybe, they live on in our hearts. I'd like to think so.

I want to remind people that sleep apnea is a serious medical condition. Left untreated, sleep apnea can leave people seriously fatigued with a sleep deficit and in other cases even cardiac arrest. Many men mistake stubbornness with stoicism and do not deal with the issue. (Remember the old newspaper obituaries where the article noted that the deceased had died in their sleep?) Women too often ignore available treatments. Years ago, many people died in their sleep because sleep apnea was not known or diagnosed. In short, if you snore or know someone who does, check it out with a medical specialist. Your friends and family will be glad you did.

Like they say, it takes a village to edit/proof a book. I'm lucky to live in a village with thoughtful people who are generous with their most valuable commodity: time. I would like to thank my volunteer readers/editors Jerry, Rabbi Alicia Magal, Bettye, Phil, and as always, my incredible life partner- Barb. I am lucky enough to be able to talk to her- my muse- my partner- my love, every night in the dark. That's where the idea for this novel first came from after one of those talks in the dark, late at night. I remember thinking how much we both treasured those talks. How would we feel if we no longer shared our life together because one of us had died? What lengths would our hearts and minds go to keep a loved one's spirit and memory alive?

I started this novel the very next day. Here's hoping we have many more nights to talk in the dark. We haven't run out of things to talk about yet. Like the book says, don't think we ever will.

Hiking on the Back Side
by Phil Finkelstein 2-14- 20

I hike the backside
After traveling backroads- the Gravel spits
And hits my car like a repetitive fist.
I leave the dirt behind-I hit the trails
My Poles, a dangling necessity,
Past the overhead electric line
A satisfying crunch Like Grape Nuts
As my boots propel forward and crush the earth's crust.
I stop to take pictures as an excuse for/to myself
Not willing to admit-I can't hike as far as I used to
I bring my shadow and my life into focus across the mini-summit.
I see the 7 Sisters- Names of Rocks don't matter- Only the
    Rocks endure,
But only if we let them
Suburban tract homes scratch like raw and open sores.
And I still walk higher-I continue and continue
Thinking I have never gone this far- But then there is this tree
Dead, broken, limbs shorn, black and still upright.
I recognize it from a photo I took years ago.
So I push forward- I see the crest-but I know as in life,
It's easier to go up than head down. I turn- and walk carefully
I watch out for the pebble that has my name on it.

Last week I fell but thankfully upwards on the trail
My feet continue down the path- crunching climbing down
No longer embarrassed at my age to slide safely on my backside.
Slowly, inexorably then I reach my car and more water.
My poles clanging as I thrust them into the back seat.
I drive home and kick off my dusty hiking boots.
I breathe in red dust and feel good.

Made in the USA
Monee, IL
29 April 2022